The Collector's Wodehouse

P. G. WODEHOUSE

# The Gold Bat

THE OVERLOOK PRESS
NEW YORK

This edition first published in the United States in 2011 by
The Overlook Press, Peter Mayer Publishers, Inc.,
141 Wooster Street, New York, NY 10012

First published by Herbert Jenkins, London, 1904
First published in the US by Macmillan, 1923

Cataloging-in-Publication Data is available from the Library of Congress

Manufactured in Germany

ISBN 978-1-59020-513-6

1 3 5 7 9 8 6 4 2

# The Gold Bat

# CONTENTS

TO

THAT PRINCE OF SLACKERS,
HERBERT WESTBROOK

'Outside!'

'Don't be an idiot, man. I bagged it first.'

'My dear chap, I've been waiting here a month.'

'When you fellows have *quite* finished rotting about in front of that bath don't let *me* detain you.'

'Anybody seen that sponge?'

'Well, look here' – this in a tone of compromise – 'let's toss for it.'

'All right. Odd man out.'

All of which, being interpreted, meant that the first match of the Easter term had just come to an end, and that those of the team who, being day boys, changed over at the pavilion, instead of performing the operation at leisure and in comfort, as did the members of houses, were discussing the vital question – who was to have first bath?

The Field Sports Committee at Wrykyn – that is, at the school which stood some half-mile outside that town and took its name from it – were not lavish in their expenditure as regarded the changing accommodation in the pavilion. Letters appeared in every second number of the *Wrykinian*, some short, others long, some from members of the school, others from Old Boys, all protesting against the condition of the first, second, and third fifteen dressing-rooms. 'Indignant' would inquire acidly, in half a page of small type, if the editor happened to be aware that there was no hair-brush in the second room, and only half a comb. 'Disgusted O. W.' would remark that when he came down with the Wandering Zephyrs to play against the third fifteen, the water supply had suddenly and mysteriously failed, and the W. Z.'s had been obliged to go home as they were, in a state of primeval grime, and he thought that this was 'a very bad thing in a school of over six hundred boys', though what the number of boys had to do with the fact that there was no water he omitted to explain. The editor would express his regret in brackets, and things would go on as before.

There was only one bath in the first fifteen room, and there were on the present occasion six claimants to it. And each claimant was of the fixed opinion that, whatever happened subsequently, he was going to have it first. Finally, on the suggestion of Otway, who had reduced tossing to a fine art, a mystic game of Tommy Dodd was played. Otway having triumphantly obtained first innings, the conversation reverted to the subject of the match.

The Easter term always opened with a scratch game against a mixed team of masters and old boys, and the school usually won without any great exertion. On this occasion the match had been rather more even than the average, and the team had only just pulled the thing off by a couple of tries to a goal. Otway expressed an opinion that the school had played badly.

'Why on earth don't you forwards let the ball out occasionally?' he asked. Otway was one of the first fifteen halves.

'They were so jolly heavy in the scrum,' said Maurice, one of the forwards. 'And when we did let it out, the outsides nearly always mucked it.'

'Well, it wasn't the halves' fault. We always got it out to the centres.'

'It wasn't the centres,' put in Robinson. 'They played awfully well. Trevor was ripping.'

'Trevor always is,' said Otway; 'I should think he's about the best captain we've had here for a long time. He's certainly one of the best centres.'

'Best there's been since Rivers-Jones,' said Clephane.

Rivers-Jones was one of those players who mark an epoch. He had been in the team fifteen years ago, and had left Wrykyn to captain Cambridge and play three years in succession for Wales. The school regarded the standard set by him as one that did not admit of comparison. However good a Wrykyn centre three-quarter might be, the most he could hope to be considered was 'the best *since* Rivers-Jones'. 'Since' Rivers-Jones, however, covered fifteen years, and to be looked on as the best centre the school could boast of during that time, meant something. For Wrykyn knew how to play football.

Since it had been decided thus that the faults in the school attack did not lie with the halves, forwards, or centres, it was more or less evident that they must be attributable to the wings. And the search for the weak spot was even further narrowed down by the general verdict that Clowes, on the left wing, had played well. With a beautiful unanimity the six occupants of the first fifteen room came to the conclusion that the man who had let the team down that day had been the man on the right – Rand-Brown, to wit, of Seymour's.

'I'll bet he doesn't stay in the first long,' said Clephane, who was now in the bath, *vice* Otway, retired. 'I suppose they had to try him, as he was the senior wing three-quarter of the second, but he's no earthly good.'

'He only got into the second because he's big,' was Robinson's opinion. 'A man who's big and strong can always get his second colours.'

'Even if he's a funk, like Rand-Brown,' said Clephane. 'Did any of you chaps notice the way he let Paget through that time he scored for them? He simply didn't attempt to tackle him. He could have brought him down like a shot if he'd only gone for him. Paget was running straight along the touch-line, and hadn't any room to dodge. I know Trevor was jolly sick about it. And then he let him through once before in just the same way in the first half, only Trevor got round and stopped him. He was rank.'

'Missed every other pass, too,' said Otway.

Clephane summed up.

'He was rank,' he said again. 'Trevor won't keep him in the team long.'

'I wish Paget hadn't left,' said Otway, referring to the wing three-quarter who, by leaving unexpectedly at the end of the Christmas term, had let Rand-Brown into the team. His loss was likely to be felt. Up till Christmas Wrykyn had done well, and Paget had been their scoring man. Rand-Brown had occupied a similar position in the second fifteen. He was big and speedy, and in second fifteen matches these qualities make up for a great deal. If a man scores one or two tries in nearly every match, people are inclined to overlook in him such failings as timidity and clumsiness. It is only when he comes to be tried in football of a higher class that he is seen through. In the second fifteen the fact that Rand-Brown was afraid to tackle his man had almost escaped notice. But the habit would not do in first fifteen circles.

'All the same,' said Clephane, pursuing his subject, 'if they don't play him, I don't see who they're going to get. He's the best of the second three-quarters, as far as I can see.'

It was this very problem that was puzzling Trevor, as he walked off the field with Paget and Clowes, when they had got into their blazers after the match. Clowes was in the same house as Trevor – Donaldson's – and Paget was staying there, too. He had been head of Donaldson's up to Christmas.

'It strikes me,' said Paget, 'the school haven't got over the holidays yet. I never saw such a lot of slackers. You ought to have taken thirty points off the sort of team you had against you today.'

'Have you ever known the school play well on the second day of term?' asked Clowes. 'The forwards always play as if the whole thing bored them to death.'

'It wasn't the forwards that mattered so much,' said Trevor. 'They'll shake down all right after a few matches. A little running and passing will put them right.'

'Let's hope so,' Paget observed, 'or we might as well scratch to Ripton at once. There's a jolly sight too much of the mince-pie and Christmas pudding about their play at present.' There was a pause. Then Paget brought out the question towards which he had been moving all the time.

'What do you think of Rand-Brown?' he asked.

It was pretty clear by the way he spoke what he thought of that player himself, but in discussing with a football captain the capabilities of the various members of his team, it is best to avoid a too positive statement one way or the other before one has heard his views on the subject. And Paget was one of those people who like to know the opinions of others before committing themselves.

Clowes, on the other hand, was in the habit of forming his

views on his own account, and expressing them. If people agreed
with them, well and good: it afforded strong presumptive evidence of their sanity. If they disagreed, it was unfortunate, but he
was not going to alter his opinions for that, unless convinced at
great length that they were unsound. He summed things up, and
gave you the result. You could take it or leave it, as you preferred.

'I thought he was bad,' said Clowes.

'Bad!' exclaimed Trevor, 'he was a disgrace. One can understand a chap having his off-days at any game, but one doesn't
expect a man in the Wrykyn first to funk. He mucked five out
of every six passes I gave him, too, and the ball wasn't a bit slip-
pery. Still, I shouldn't mind that so much if he had only gone for
his man properly. It isn't being out of practice that makes you
funk. And even when he did have a try at you, Paget, he always
went high.'

'That,' said Clowes thoughtfully, 'would seem to show that he
was game.'

Nobody so much as smiled. Nobody ever did smile at Clowes'
essays in wit, perhaps because of the solemn, almost sad, tone of
voice in which he delivered them. He was tall and dark and thin,
and had a pensive eye, which encouraged the more soulful of
his female relatives to entertain hopes that he would some day
take orders.

'Well,' said Paget, relieved at finding that he did not stand
alone in his views on Rand-Brown's performance, 'I must say
I thought he was awfully bad myself.'

'I shall try somebody else next match,' said Trevor. 'It'll be
rather hard, though. The man one would naturally put in, Bryce,
left at Christmas, worse luck.'

Bryce was the other wing three-quarter of the second fifteen.

'Isn't there anybody in the third?' asked Paget.

'Barry,' said Clowes briefly.

'Clowes thinks Barry's good,' explained Trevor.

'He *is* good,' said Clowes. 'I admit he's small, but he can tackle.'

'The question is, would he be any good in the first? A chap might do jolly well for the third, and still not be worth trying for the first.'

'I don't remember much about Barry,' said Paget, 'except being collared by him when we played Seymour's last year in the final. I certainly came away with a sort of impression that he could tackle. I thought he marked me jolly well.'

'There you are, then,' said Clowes. 'A year ago Barry could tackle Paget. There's no reason for supposing that he's fallen off since then. We've seen that Rand-Brown *can't* tackle Paget. Ergo, Barry is better worth playing for the team than Rand-Brown. Q.E.D.'

'All right, then,' replied Trevor. 'There can't be any harm in trying him. We'll have another scratch game on Thursday. Will you be here then, Paget?'

'Oh, yes. I'm stopping till Saturday.'

'Good man. Then we shall be able to see how he does against you. I wish you hadn't left, though, by Jove. We should have had Ripton on toast, the same as last term.'

Wrykyn played five schools, but six school matches. The school that they played twice in the season was Ripton. To win one Ripton match meant that, however many losses it might have sustained in the other matches, the school had had, at any rate, a passable season. To win two Ripton matches in the same year was almost unheard of. This year there had seemed every likelihood of it. The match before Christmas on the Ripton ground had resulted in a win for Wrykyn by two goals and a try to a try. But the calculations of the school had been upset by the sudden departure of Paget at the end of term, and also of Bryce, who had hitherto been regarded as his understudy. And in the first Ripton match the two goals had both been scored by Paget, and both had been brilliant bits of individual play, which a lesser man could not have carried through.

The conclusion, therefore, at which the school reluctantly arrived, was that their chances of winning the second match could not be judged by their previous success. They would have to approach the Easter term fixture from another – a non-Paget – standpoint. In these circumstances it became a serious problem: who was to get the fifteenth place? Whoever played in Paget's stead against Ripton would be certain, if the match were won, to receive his colours. Who, then, would fill the vacancy?

'Rand-Brown, of course,' said the crowd.

But the experts, as we have shown, were of a different opinion.

Trevor did not take long to resume a garb of civilisation. He never wasted much time over anything. He was gifted with a boundless energy, which might possibly have made him unpopular had he not justified it by results. The football of the school had never been in such a flourishing condition as it had attained to on his succeeding to the captaincy. It was not only that the first fifteen was good. The excellence of a first fifteen does not always depend on the captain. But the games, even down to the very humblest junior game, had woken up one morning – at the beginning of the previous term – to find themselves, much to their surprise, organised going concerns. Like the immortal Captain Pott, Trevor was 'a terror to the shirker and the lubber'. And the resemblance was further increased by the fact that he was 'a toughish lot', who was 'little, but steel and india-rubber'. At first sight his appearance was not imposing. Paterfamilias, who had heard his son's eulogies on Trevor's performances during the holidays, and came down to watch the school play a match, was generally rather disappointed on seeing five feet six where he had looked for at least six foot one, and ten stone where he had expected thirteen. But then, what there was of Trevor was, as previously remarked, steel and india-rubber, and he certainly played football like a miniature Stoddart. It was characteristic of him that, though this was the first match of the term, his condition seemed to be as good as possible. He had done all his own work on the field and most of Rand-Brown's, and apparently had not turned a hair. He was one of those conscientious people who train in the holidays.

When he had changed, he went down the passage to Clowes' study. Clowes was in the position he frequently took up when the weather was good – wedged into his window in a sitting position, one leg in the study, the other hanging outside over space. The indoor leg lacked a boot, so that it was evident that its owner had at least had the energy to begin to change. That he had given the thing up after that, exhausted with the effort, was what one naturally expected from Clowes. He would have made a splendid actor: he was so good at resting.

'Hurry up and dress,' said Trevor; 'I want you to come over to the baths.'

'What on earth do you want over at the baths?'

'I want to see O'Hara.'

'Oh, yes, I remember. Dexter's are camping out there, aren't they? I heard they were. Why is it?'

'One of the Dexter kids got measles in the last week of the holidays, so they shunted all the beds and things across, and the chaps went back there instead of to the house.'

In the winter term the baths were always boarded over and converted into a sort of extra gymnasium where you could go and box or fence when there was no room to do it in the real gymnasium. Socker and stump-cricket were also largely played there, the floor being admirably suited to such games, though the light was always rather tricky, and prevented heavy scoring.

'I should think,' said Clowes, 'from what I've seen of Dexter's beauties, that Dexter would like them to camp out at the bottom

of the baths all the year round. It would be a happy release for him
if they were all drowned. And I suppose if he had to choose any
one of them for a violent death, he'd pick O'Hara. O'Hara must
be a boon to a house-master. I've known chaps break rules when
the spirit moved them, but he's the only one I've met who breaks
them all day long and well into the night simply for amusement.
I've often thought of writing to the S.P.C.A. about it. I suppose
you could call Dexter an animal all right?'

'O'Hara's right enough, really. A man like Dexter would make
any fellow run amuck. And then O'Hara's an Irishman to start
with, which makes a difference.'

There is usually one house in every school of the black sheep
sort, and, if you go to the root of the matter, you will generally
find that the fault is with the master of that house. A house-
master who enters into the life of his house, coaches them in
games – if an athlete – or, if not an athlete, watches the games,
umpiring at cricket and refereeing at football, never finds much
difficulty in keeping order. It may be accepted as fact that the
juniors of a house will never be orderly of their own free will,
but disturbances in the junior day-room do not make the house
undisciplined. The prefects are the criterion. If you find them
joining in the general 'rags', and even starting private ones on
their own account, then you may safely say that it is time the
master of that house retired from the business, and took to
chicken-farming. And that was the state of things in Dexter's.
It was the most lawless of the houses. Mr Dexter belonged to a
type of master almost unknown at a public school – the usher
type. In a private school he might have passed. At Wrykyn he
was out of place. To him the whole duty of a house-master
appeared to be to wage war against his house.

When Dexter's won the final for the cricket cup in the summer term of two years back, the match lasted four afternoons – four solid afternoons of glorious, up-and-down cricket. Mr Dexter did not see a single ball of that match bowled. He was prowling in sequestered lanes and broken-down barns out of bounds on the off-chance that he might catch some member of his house smoking there. As if the whole of the house, from the head to the smallest fag, were not on the field watching Day's best bats collapse before Henderson's bowling, and Moriarty hit up that marvellous and unexpected fifty-three at the end of the second innings!

That sort of thing definitely stamps a master.

'What do you want to see O'Hara about?' asked Clowes.

'He's got my little gold bat. I lent it him in the holidays.'

A remark which needs a footnote. The bat referred to was made of gold, and was about an inch long by an eighth broad. It had come into existence some ten years previously, in the following manner. The inter-house cricket cup at Wrykyn had originally been a rather tarnished and unimpressive vessel, whose only merit consisted in the fact that it was of silver. Ten years ago an Old Wrykinian, suddenly reflecting that it would not be a bad idea to do something for the school in a small way, hied him to the nearest jeweller's and purchased another silver cup, vast withal and cunningly decorated with filigree work, and standing on a massive ebony plinth, round which were little silver lozenges just big enough to hold the name of the winning house and the year of grace. This he presented with his blessing to be competed for by the dozen houses that made up the school of Wrykyn, and it was formally established as the house cricket cup. The question now arose: what was to be done with the other cup? The School House, who happened to be the holders at the time, suggested disinterestedly that it should become the property of the house which had won it last. 'Not so,' replied the Field Sports Committee, 'but far otherwise. We will have it melted down in a fiery furnace, and thereafter fashioned into eleven little silver bats. And these little silver bats shall be the guerdon of the eleven members of the winning team, to have and to hold for the space of one year, unless, by winning the cup twice in succession, they gain the right of keeping the bat for yet another year. How is that, umpire?' And the authorities replied, 'O men of infinite resource and sagacity, verily is it a cold day when *you* get left behind. Forge ahead.' But, when they had forged ahead, behold! it would not run to eleven little silver bats, but only to ten little silver bats. Thereupon the headmaster, a man liberal with his cash, caused an eleventh little bat to be fashioned – for the captain of the winning team to have and to hold in the manner aforesaid. And, to single it out from the others, it was wrought, not of silver, but of gold. And so it came to pass that at the time of our story Trevor was in possession of the little gold bat, because Donaldson's had won the cup in the previous summer, and he had captained them – and, incidentally, had scored seventy-five without a mistake.

'Well, I'm hanged if I would trust O'Hara with my bat,' said Clowes, referring to the silver ornament on his own watch-chain; 'he's probably pawned yours in the holidays. Why did you lend it to him?'

'His people wanted to see it. I know him at home, you know. They asked me to lunch the last day but one of the holidays, and we got talking about the bat, because, of course, if we hadn't beaten Dexter's in the final, O'Hara would have had it himself. So I sent it over next day with a note asking O'Hara to bring it back with him here.'

'Oh, well, there's a chance, then, seeing he's only had it so little time, that he hasn't pawned it yet. You'd better rush off and get it back as soon as possible. It's no good waiting for me. I shan't be ready for weeks.'

'Where's Paget?'

'Teaing with Donaldson. At least, he said he was going to.'

'Then I suppose I shall have to go alone. I hate walking alone.'

'If you hurry,' said Clowes, scanning the road from his post of vantage, 'you'll be able to go with your fascinating pal Ruthven. He's just gone out.'

Trevor dashed downstairs in his energetic way, and overtook the youth referred to.

Clowes brooded over them from above like a sorrowful and rather disgusted Providence. Trevor's liking for Ruthven, who was a Donaldsonite like himself, was one of the few points on which the two had any real disagreement. Clowes could not understand how any person in his senses could of his own free will make an intimate friend of Ruthven.

'Hullo, Trevor,' said Ruthven.

'Come over to the baths,' said Trevor, 'I want to see O'Hara about something. Or were you going somewhere else?'

'I wasn't going anywhere in particular. I never know what to do in term-time. It's deadly dull.'

Trevor could never understand how any one could find term-time dull. For his own part, there always seemed too much to do in the time.

'You aren't allowed to play games?' he said, remembering something about a doctor's certificate in the past.

'No,' said Ruthven. 'Thank goodness,' he added.

Which remark silenced Trevor. To a person who thanked goodness that he was not allowed to play games he could find nothing to say. But he ceased to wonder how it was that Ruthven was dull.

They proceeded to the baths together in silence. O'Hara, they were informed by a Dexter's fag who met them outside the door, was not about.

'When he comes back,' said Trevor, 'tell him I want him to come to tea tomorrow directly after school, and bring my bat. Don't forget.'

The fag promised to make a point of it.

One of the rules that governed the life of Donough O'Hara, the light-hearted descendant of the O'Haras of Castle Tater-fields, Co. Clare, Ireland, was 'Never refuse the offer of a free tea'. So, on receipt – per the Dexter's fag referred to – of Trevor's invitation, he scratched one engagement (with his mathematical master – not wholly unconnected with the working-out of Examples 200 to 206 in Hall and Knight's Algebra), postponed another (with his friend and ally Moriarty, of Dexter's, who wished to box with him in the gymnasium), and made his way at a leisurely pace towards Donaldson's. He was feeling particularly pleased with himself today, for several reasons. He had begun the day well by scoring brilliantly off Mr Dexter across the matutinal rasher and coffee. In morning school he had been put on to trans-late the one passage which he happened to have prepared – the first ten lines, in fact, of the hundred which formed the morning's lesson. And in the final hour of afternoon school, which was devoted to French, he had discovered and exploited with great success an entirely new and original form of ragging. This, he felt, was the strenuous life; this was living one's life as one's life should be lived.

He met Trevor at the gate. As they were going in, a carriage and pair dashed past. Its cargo consisted of two people, the headmaster, looking bored, and a small, dapper man, with a very red face, who looked excited, and was talking volubly. Trevor and O'Hara raised their caps as the chariot swept by, but the salute passed unnoticed. The Head appeared to be wrapped in thought.

'What's the Old Man doing in a carriage, I wonder,' said Trevor, looking after them. 'Who's that with him?'

'That,' said O'Hara, 'is Sir Eustace Briggs.'

'Who's Sir Eustace Briggs?'

O'Hara explained, in a rich brogue, that Sir Eustace was Mayor of Wrykyn, a keen politician, and a hater of the Irish nation, judging by his letters and speeches.

They went into Trevor's study. Clowes was occupying the window in his usual manner.

'Hullo, O'Hara,' he said, 'there is an air of quiet satisfaction about you that seems to show that you've been ragging Dexter. Have you?'

'Oh, that was only this morning at breakfast. The best rag was in French,' replied O'Hara, who then proceeded to explain in detail the methods he had employed to embitter the existence of the hapless Gallic exile with whom he had come in contact. It was that gentleman's custom to sit on a certain desk while conducting the lesson. This desk chanced to be O'Hara's. On the principle that a man may do what he likes with his own, he had entered the room privily in the dinner-hour, and removed the screws from his desk, with the result that for the first half-hour of the lesson the class had been occupied in excavating M. Gandinois from the ruins. That gentleman's first act on regaining his equilibrium had been to send O'Hara out of the room, and O'Hara, who had foreseen this emergency, had spent a very pleasant half-hour in the passage with some mixed chocolates and a copy of Mr Hornung's *Amateur Cracksman*. It was his notion of a cheerful and instructive French lesson.

'What were you talking about when you came in?' asked Clowes. 'Who's been slanging Ireland, O'Hara?'

'The man Briggs.'

'What are you going to do about it? Aren't you going to take any steps?'

'Is it steps?' said O'Hara, warmly, 'and haven't we—'

He stopped.

'Well?'

'Ye know,' he said, seriously, 'ye mustn't let it go any further. I shall get sacked if it's found out. An' so will Moriarty, too.'

'Why?' asked Trevor, looking up from the tea-pot he was filling, 'what on earth have you been doing?'

'Wouldn't it be rather a cheery idea,' suggested Clowes, 'if you began at the beginning.'

'Well, ye see,' O'Hara began, 'it was this way. The first I heard of it was from Dexter. He was trying to score off me as usual, an' he said, "Have ye seen the paper this morning, O'Hara?" I said, no, I had not. Then he said, "Ah," he said, "ye should look at it. There's something there that ye'll find interesting." I said, "Yes, sir?" in me respectful way. "Yes," said he, "the Irish members have been making their customary disturbances in the House. Why is it, O'Hara," he said, "that Irishmen are always thrusting themselves forward and making disturbances for purposes of self-advertisement?" "Why, indeed, sir?" said I, not knowing what else to say, and after that the conversation ceased.'

'Go on,' said Clowes.

'After breakfast Moriarty came to me with a paper, and showed me what they had been saying about the Irish. There was a letter from the man Briggs on the subject. "A very sensible and temperate letter from Sir Eustace Briggs", they called it, but bedad! if that was a temperate letter, I should like to know what an intemperate one is. Well, we read it through, and Moriarty said to me, "Can we let this stay as it is?" And I said, "No. We can't." "Well," said Moriarty to me, "what are we to do about it? I should like to tar and feather the man," he said. "We can't do that," I said, "but why not tar and feather his statue?" I said. So we thought we would. Ye know where the statue is, I suppose? It's in the Recreation Ground just across the river.'

'I know the place,' said Clowes. 'Go on. This is ripping. I always knew you were pretty mad, but this sounds as if it were going to beat all previous records.'

'Have ye seen the baths this term,' continued O'Hara, 'since they shifted Dexter's house into them? The beds are in two long rows along each wall. Moriarty's and mine are the last two at the end farthest from the door.'

'Just under the gallery,' said Trevor. 'I see.'

'That's it. Well, at half-past ten sharp every night Dexter sees that we're all in, locks the door, and goes off to sleep at the Old Man's, and we don't see him again till breakfast. He turns the gas off from outside. At half-past seven the next morning, Smith' – Smith was one of the school porters – 'unlocks the door and calls us, and we go over to the Hall to breakfast.'

'Well?'

'Well, directly everybody was asleep last night – it wasn't till after one, as there was a rag on – Moriarty and I got up, dressed, and climbed up into the gallery. Ye know the gallery windows? They open at the top, an' it's rather hard to get out of them. But we managed it, and dropped on to the gravel outside.'

'Long drop,' said Clowes.

'Yes. I hurt myself rather. But it was in a good cause. I dropped first, and while I was on the ground, Moriarty came on top of me. That's how I got hurt. But it wasn't much, and we cut across the grounds, and over the fence, and down to the river. It was a fine night, and not very dark, and everything smelt ripping down by the river.'

'Don't get poetical,' said Clowes. 'Stick to the point.'

'We got into the boat-house—'

'How?' asked the practical Trevor, for the boat-house was wont to be locked at one in the morning.

'Moriarty had a key that fitted,' explained O'Hara, briefly. 'We got in, and launched a boat – a big tub – put in the tar and a couple of brushes – there's always tar in the boat-house – and rowed across.'

'Wait a bit,' interrupted Trevor, 'you said tar and feathers. Where did you get the feathers?'

'We used leaves. They do just as well, and there were heaps on the bank. Well, when we landed, we tied up the boat, and bucked across to the Recreation Ground. We got over the railings – beastly, spiky railings – and went over to the statue. Ye know where the statue stands? It's right in the middle of the place, where everybody can see it. Moriarty got up first, and I handed him the tar and a brush. Then I went up with the other brush, and we began. We did his face first. It was too dark to see really well, but I think we made a good job of it. When we had put about as much tar on as we thought would do, we took out the leaves – which we were carrying in our pockets – and spread them on. Then we did the rest of him, and after about half an hour, when we thought we'd done about enough, we got into our boat again, and came back.'

'And what did you do till half-past seven?'

'We couldn't get back the way we'd come, so we slept in the boat-house.'

'Well – I'm – hanged,' was Trevor's comment on the story. Clowes roared with laughter. O'Hara was a perpetual joy to him.

As O'Hara was going, Trevor asked him for his gold bat.

'You haven't lost it, I hope?' he said.

O'Hara felt in his pocket, but brought his hand out at once and transferred it to another pocket. A look of anxiety came over his face, and was reflected in Trevor's.

'I could have sworn it was in that pocket,' he said.

'You *haven't* lost it?' queried Trevor again.

'He has,' said Clowes, confidently. 'If you want to know where that bat is, I should say you'd find it somewhere between the baths and the statue. At the foot of the statue, for choice. It seems to me – correct me if I am wrong – that you have been and gone and done it, me broth av a bhoy.'

O'Hara gave up the search.

'It's gone,' he said. 'Man, I'm most awfully sorry. I'd sooner have lost a ten-pound note.'

'I don't see why you should lose either,' snapped Trevor. 'Why the blazes can't you be more careful.'

O'Hara was too penitent for words. Clowes took it on himself to point out the bright side.

'There's nothing to get sick about, really,' he said. 'If the thing doesn't turn up, though it probably will, you'll simply have to tell the Old Man that it's lost. He'll have another made. You won't be asked for it till just before Sports Day either, so you will have plenty of time to find it.'

The challenge cups, and also the bats, had to be given to the authorities before the sports, to be formally presented on Sports Day.

'Oh, I suppose it'll be all right,' said Trevor, 'but I hope it won't be found anywhere near the statue.'

O'Hara said he hoped so too.

The team to play in any match was always put upon the notice-board at the foot of the stairs in the senior block a day before the date of the fixture. Both first and second fifteens had matches on the Thursday of this week. The second were playing a team brought down by an old Wrykinian. The first had a scratch game.

When Barry, accompanied by M'Todd, who shared his study at Seymour's and rarely left him for two minutes on end, passed by the notice-board at the quarter to eleven interval, it was to the second fifteen list that he turned his attention. Now that Bryce had left, he thought he might have a chance of getting into the second. His only real rival, he considered, was Crawford, of the School House, who was the other wing three-quarter of the third fifteen. The first name he saw on the list was Crawford's. It seemed to be written twice as large as any of the others, and his own was nowhere to be seen. The fact that he had half expected the calamity made things no better. He had set his heart on playing for the second this term.

Then suddenly he noticed a remarkable phenomenon. The other wing three-quarter was Rand-Brown. If Rand-Brown was playing for the second, who was playing for the first?

He looked at the list.

'*Come* on,' he said hastily to M'Todd. He wanted to get away somewhere where his agitated condition would not be noticed. He felt quite faint at the shock of seeing his name on the list of the first fifteen. There it was, however, as large as life. 'M. Barry.' Separated from the rest by a thin red line, but still there. In his most optimistic moments he had never dreamed of this. M'Todd was reading slowly through the list of the second. He did everything slowly, except eating.

'Come on,' said Barry again.

M'Todd had, after much deliberation, arrived at a profound truth. He turned to Barry, and imparted his discovery to him in the weighty manner of one who realises the importance of his words.

'Look here,' he said, 'your name's not down here.'

'I know. *Come* on.'

'But that means you're not playing for the second.'

'Of course it does. Well, if you aren't coming, I'm off.'

'But, look here—'

Barry disappeared through the door. After a moment's pause, M'Todd followed him. He came up with him on the senior gravel.

'What's up?' he inquired.

'Nothing,' said Barry.

'Are you sick about not playing for the second?'

'No.'

'You are, really. Come and have a bun.'

In the philosophy of M'Todd it was indeed a deep-rooted sorrow that could not be cured by the internal application of a new, hot bun. It had never failed in his own case.

'Bun!' Barry was quite shocked at the suggestion. 'I can't afford to get myself out of condition with beastly buns.'

'But if you aren't playing—'

'You ass. I'm playing for the first. Now, do you see?'

M'Todd gaped. His mind never worked very rapidly.

'What about Rand-Brown, then?' he said.

'Rand-Brown's been chucked out. Can't you understand? You *are* an idiot. Rand-Brown's playing for the second, and I'm playing for the first.'

'But you're—'

He stopped. He had been going to point out that Barry's tender years – he was only sixteen – and smallness would make it impossible for him to play with success for the first fifteen. He refrained owing to a conviction that the remark would not be wholly judicious. Barry was touchy on the subject of his size, and M'Todd had suffered before now for commenting on it in a disparaging spirit.

'I tell you what we'll do after school,' said Barry, 'we'll have some running and passing. It'll do you a lot of good, and I want to practise taking passes at full speed. You can trot along at your ordinary pace, and I'll sprint up from behind.'

M'Todd saw no objection to that. Trotting along at his ordinary pace – five miles an hour – would just suit him.

'Then after that,' continued Barry, with a look of enthusiasm, 'I want to practise passing back to my centre. Paget used to do it awfully well last term, and I know Trevor expects his wing to. So I'll buck along, and you race up to take my pass. See?'

This was not in M'Todd's line at all. He proposed a slight alteration in the scheme.

'Hadn't you better get somebody else—?' he began.

'Don't be a slack beast,' said Barry. 'You want exercise awfully badly.'

And, as M'Todd always did exactly as Barry wished, he gave in, and spent from four-thirty to five that afternoon in the prescribed manner. A suggestion on his part at five sharp that it wouldn't be a bad idea to go and have some tea was not favourably received by the enthusiastic three-quarter, who proposed to devote what time remained before lock-up to practising drop-kicking. It was a painful alternative that faced M'Todd. His allegiance to Barry demanded that he should consent to the scheme. On the other hand, his allegiance to afternoon tea – equally strong – called him back to the house, where there was cake, and also muffins. In the end the question was solved by the appearance of Drummond, of Seymour's, garbed in football things, and also anxious to practise drop-kicking. So M'Todd was dismissed to his tea with opprobrious epithets, and Barry and Drummond settled down to a little serious and scientific work.

Making allowances for the inevitable attack of nerves that attends a first appearance in higher football circles than one is accustomed to, Barry did well against the scratch team – certainly far better than Rand-Brown had done. His smallness was, of course, against him, and, on the only occasion on which he really got away, Paget overtook him and brought him down. But then Paget was exceptionally fast. In the two most important branches of the game, the taking of passes and tackling, Barry did well. As far as pluck went he had enough for two, and when the whistle blew for no-side he had not let Paget through once, and Trevor felt that his inclusion in the team had been justified. There was another scratch game on the Saturday. Barry played in it, and did much better. Paget had gone away by an early train, and the man he had to mark now was one of the masters, who had been good in his time, but was getting a trifle old for football. Barry scored twice, and on one occasion, by passing back to Trevor after the manner of Paget, enabled the captain to run in. And Trevor, like the captain in *Billy Taylor*, 'werry much approved of what he'd done'. Barry began to be regarded in the school as a regular member of the fifteen. The first of the fixture-card matches, versus the Town, was due on the following Saturday, and it was generally expected that he would play. M'Todd's devotion increased every day. He even went to the length of taking long runs with him. And if there was one thing in the world that M'Todd loathed, it was a long run.

On the Thursday before the match against the Town, Clowes came chuckling to Trevor's study after preparation, and asked him if he had heard the latest.

'Have you ever heard of the League?' he said.

Trevor pondered.

'I don't think so,' he replied.

'How long have you been at the school?'

'Let's see. It'll be five years at the end of the summer term.'

'Ah, then you wouldn't remember. I've been here a couple of terms longer than you, and the row about the League was in my first term.'

'What was the row?'

'Oh, only some chaps formed a sort of secret society in the place. Kind of Vehmgericht, you know. If they got their knife into any one, he usually got beans, and could never find out where they came from. At first, as a matter of fact, the thing was quite a philanthropical concern. There used to be a good deal of bullying in the place then – at least, in some of the houses – and, as the prefects couldn't or wouldn't stop it, some fellows started this League.'

'Did it work?'

'Work! By Jove, I should think it did. Chaps who previously couldn't get through the day without making some wretched kid's life not worth living used to go about as nervous as cats, looking over their shoulders every other second. There was one man in particular, a chap called Leigh. He was hauled out of bed one night, blindfolded, and ducked in a cold bath. He was in the School House.'

'Why did the League bust up?'

'Well, partly because the fellows left, but chiefly because they didn't stick to the philanthropist idea. If anybody did anything they didn't like, they used to go for him. At last they put their foot into it badly. A chap called Robinson – in this house by the way – offended them in some way, and one morning he was found tied up in the bath, up to his neck in cold water. Apparently he'd been there about an hour. He got pneumonia, and almost died, and then the authorities began to get going. Robinson thought he had recognised the voice of one of the chaps – I forget his name. The chap was had up by the Old Man, and gave the show away entirely. About a dozen fellows were sacked, clean off the reel. Since then the thing has been dropped.'

'But what about it? What were you going to say when you came in?'

'Why, it's been revived!'

'Rot!'

'It's a fact. Do you know Mill, a prefect, in Seymour's?'

'Only by sight.'

'I met him just now. He's in a raving condition. His study's been wrecked. You never saw such a sight. Everything upside down or smashed. He has been showing me the ruins.'

'I believe Mill is awfully barred in Seymour's,' said Trevor. 'Anybody might have ragged his study.'

That's just what I thought. He's just the sort of man the League used to go for.'

'That doesn't prove that it's been revived, all the same,' objected Trevor.

'No, friend; but this does. Mill found it tied to a chair.'

It was a small card. It looked like an ordinary visiting card. On it, in neat print, were the words, '*With the compliments of the League*'.

'That's exactly the same sort of card as they used to use,' said Clowes. 'I've seen some of them. What do you think of that?'

'I think whoever has started the thing is a pretty average-sized idiot. He's bound to get caught some time or other, and then out he goes. The Old Man wouldn't think twice about sacking a chap of that sort.'

'A chap of that sort,' said Clowes, 'will take jolly good care he isn't caught. But it's rather sport, isn't it?'

And he went off to his study.

Next day there was further evidence that the League was an actual going concern. When Trevor came down to breakfast, he found a letter by his plate. It was printed, as the card had been. It was signed 'The President of the League'. And the purport of it was that the League did not wish Barry to continue to play for the first fifteen.

Trevor's first idea was that somebody had sent the letter for a joke, – Clowes for choice.

He sounded him on the subject after breakfast.

'Did you send me that letter?' he inquired, when Clowes came into his study to borrow a *Sportsman*.

'What letter? Did you send the team for tomorrow up to the sporter? I wonder what sort of a lot the Town are bringing.'

'About not giving Barry his footer colours?'

Clowes was reading the paper.

'Giving whom?' he asked.

'Barry. Can't you listen?'

'Giving him what?'

'Footer colours.'

'What about them?'

Trevor sprang at the paper, and tore it away from him. After which he sat on the fragments.

'Did you send me a letter about not giving Barry his footer colours?'

Clowes surveyed him with the air of a nurse to whom the family baby has just said some more than usually good thing.

'Don't stop,' he said, 'I could listen all day.'

Trevor felt in his pocket for the note, and flung it at him. Clowes picked it up, and read it gravely.

'What *are* footer colours?' he asked.

'Well,' said Trevor, 'it's a pretty rotten sort of joke, whoever sent it. You haven't said yet whether you did or not.'

'What earthly reason should I have for sending it? And I think you're making a mistake if you think this is meant as a joke.'

'You don't really believe this League rot?'

'You didn't see Mill's study "after treatment". I did. Anyhow, how do you account for the card I showed you?'

'But that sort of thing doesn't happen at school.'

'Well, it *has* happened, you see.'

'Who do you think did send the letter, then?'

'The President of the League.'

'And who the dickens is the President of the League when he's at home?'

'If I knew that, I should tell Mill, and earn his blessing. Not that I want it.'

'Then, I suppose,' snorted Trevor, 'you'd suggest that on the strength of this letter I'd better leave Barry out of the team?'

'Satirically in brackets,' commented Clowes.

'It's no good your jumping on *me*,' he added. 'I've done nothing. All I suggest is that you'd better keep more or less of a lookout. If this League's anything like the old one, you'll find they've all sorts of ways of getting at people they don't love. I shouldn't like to come down for a bath some morning, and find you already in possession, tied up like Robinson. When they found Robinson, he was quite blue both as to the face and speech. He didn't speak very clearly, but what one could catch was well worth hearing. I should advise you to sleep with a loaded revolver under your pillow.'

'The first thing I shall do is find out who wrote this letter.'

'I should,' said Clowes, encouragingly. 'Keep moving.'

In Seymour's house the Mill's study incident formed the only theme of conversation that morning. Previously the sudden elevation to the first fifteen of Barry, who was popular in the house, at the expense of Rand-Brown, who was unpopular, had given Seymour's something to talk about. But the ragging of the study put this topic entirely in the shade. The study was still on view in almost its original condition of disorder, and all day comparative strangers flocked to see Mill in his den, in order to inspect things. Mill was a youth with few friends, and it is probable that more of his fellow-Seymourites crossed the threshold of his study on the day after the occurrence than had visited him in the entire course of his school career. Brown would come in to borrow a knife, would sweep the room with one comprehensive glance, and depart, to be followed at brief intervals by Smith, Robinson, and Jones, who came respectively to learn the right time, to borrow a book, and to ask him if he had seen a pencil anywhere. Towards the end of the day, Mill would seem to have wearied somewhat of the proceedings, as was proved when Master Thomas Renford, aged fourteen (who fagged for Milton, the head of the house), burst in on the thin pretence that he had mistaken the study for that of his rightful master, and gave vent to a prolonged whistle of surprise and satisfaction at the sight of the ruins. On that occasion, the incensed owner of the dismantled study, taking a mean advantage of the fact that he was a prefect, and so entitled to wield the rod, produced a handy swagger-stick from an adjacent corner, and, inviting Master Renford to bend over, gave him six of the best to remember him by. Which ceremony being concluded, he kicked him out into the passage, and Renford went down to the junior day-room to tell his friend Harvey about it.

'Gave me six, the cad,' said he, 'just because I had a look at his beastly study. Why shouldn't I look at his study if I like? I've a jolly good mind to go up and have another squint.'

Harvey warmly approved the scheme.

'No, I don't think I will,' said Renford with a yawn. 'It's such a fag going upstairs.'

'Yes, isn't it?' said Harvey.

'And he's such a beast, too.'

'Yes, isn't he?' said Harvey.

'I'm jolly glad his study *has* been ragged,' continued the vindictive Renford.

'It's jolly exciting, isn't it?' added Harvey. 'And I thought this term was going to be slow. The Easter term generally is.'

This remark seemed to suggest a train of thought to Renford, who made the following cryptic observation. 'Have you seen them today?'

To the ordinary person the words would have conveyed little meaning. To Harvey they appeared to teem with import.

'Yes,' he said, 'I saw them early this morning.'

'Were they all right?'

'Yes. Splendid.'

'Good,' said Renford.

Barry's friend Drummond was one of those who had visited the scene of the disaster early, before Mill's energetic hand had repaired the damage done, and his narrative was consequently in some demand.

'The place was in a frightful muck,' he said. 'Everything smashed except the table; and ink all over the place. Whoever did it must have been fairly sick with him, or he'd never have taken the trouble to do it so thoroughly. Made a fair old hash of things, didn't he, Bertie?'

'Bertie' was the form in which the school elected to serve up

the name of De Bertini. Raoul de Bertini was a French boy who
had come to Wrykyn in the previous term. Drummond's father
had met his father in Paris, and Drummond was supposed to be
looking after Bertie. They shared a study together. Bertie could
not speak much English, and what he did speak was, like Mill's
furniture, badly broken.

'Pardon?' he said.

'Doesn't matter,' said Drummond, 'it wasn't anything important. I was only appealing to you for corroborative detail to give
artistic verisimilitude to a bald and unconvincing narrative.'

Bertie grinned politely. He always grinned when he was not
quite equal to the intellectual pressure of the conversation. As a
consequence of which, he was generally, like Mrs Fezziwig, one
vast, substantial smile.

'I never liked Mill much,' said Barry, 'but I think it's rather
bad luck on the man.'

'Once,' announced M'Todd, solemnly, 'he kicked me – for
making a row in the passage.' It was plain that the recollection
rankled.

Barry would probably have pointed out what an excellent
and praiseworthy act on Mill's part that had been, when Rand-
Brown came in.

'Prefects' meeting?' he inquired. 'Or haven't they made you a
prefect yet, M'Todd?'

M'Todd said they had not.

Nobody present liked Rand-Brown, and they looked at him
rather inquiringly, as if to ask what he had come for. A friend may
drop in for a chat. An acquaintance must justify his intrusion.

Rand-Brown ignored the silent inquiry. He seated himself on
the table, and dragged up a chair to rest his legs on.

'Talking about Mill, of course?' he said.

'Yes,' said Drummond. 'Have you seen his study since it happened?'

'Yes.'

Rand-Brown smiled, as if the recollection amused him. He was one of those people who do not look their best when they smile.

'Playing for the first tomorrow, Barry?'

'I don't know,' said Barry, shortly. 'I haven't seen the list.'

He objected to the introduction of the topic. It is never pleasant to have to discuss games with the very man one has ousted from the team.

Drummond, too, seemed to feel that the situation was an embarrassing one, for a few minutes later he got up to go over to the gymnasium.

'Any of you chaps coming?' he asked.

Barry and M'Todd thought they would, and the three left the room.

'Nothing like showing a man you don't want him, eh, Bertie? What do you think?' said Rand-Brown.

Bertie grinned politely.

The most immediate effect of telling anybody not to do a thing is to make him do it, in order to assert his independence. Trevor's first act on receipt of the letter was to include Barry in the team against the Town. It was what he would have done in any case, but, under the circumstances, he felt a peculiar pleasure in doing it. The incident also had the effect of recalling to his mind the fact that he had tried Barry in the first instance on his own responsibility, without consulting the committee. The committee of the first fifteen consisted of the two old colours who came immediately after the captain on the list. The powers of a committee varied according to the determination and truculence of the members of it. On any definite and important step, affecting the welfare of the fifteen, the captain theoretically could not move without their approval. But if the captain happened to be strong-minded and the committee weak, they were apt to be slightly out of it, and the captain would develop a habit of consulting them a day or so after he had done a thing. He would give a man his colours, and inform the committee of it on the following afternoon, when the thing was done and could not be repealed.

Trevor was accustomed to ask the advice of his lieutenants fairly frequently. He never gave colours, for instance, off his own bat. It seemed to him that it might be as well to learn what views Milton and Allardyce had on the subject of Barry, and, after the Town team had gone back across the river, defeated by a goal and a try to nil, he changed and went over to Seymour's to interview Milton.

Milton was in an arm-chair, watching Renford brew tea. His was one of the few studies in the school in which there was an arm-chair. With the majority of his contemporaries, it would only run to the portable kind that fold up.

'Come and have some tea, Trevor,' said Milton.

'Thanks. If there's any going.'

'Heaps. Is there anything to eat, Renford?'

The fag, appealed to on this important point, pondered darkly for a moment.

'There *was* some cake,' he said.

'That's all right,' interrupted Milton, cheerfully. 'Scratch the cake. I ate it before the match. Isn't there anything else?'

Milton had a healthy appetite.

'Then there used to be some biscuits.'

'Biscuits are off. I finished 'em yesterday. Look here, young Renford, what you'd better do is cut across to the shop and get some more cake and some more biscuits, and tell 'em to put it down to me. And don't be long.'

'A miles better idea would be to send him over to Donaldson's to fetch something from my study,' suggested Trevor. 'It isn't nearly so far, and I've got heaps of stuff.'

'Ripping. Cut over to Donaldson's, young Renford. As a matter of fact,' he added, confidentially, when the emissary had vanished, 'I'm not half sure that the other dodge would have worked. They seem to think at the shop that I've had about enough things on tick lately. I haven't settled up for last term yet.

I've spent all I've got on this study. What do you think of those photographs?'

Trevor got up and inspected them. They filled the mantelpiece and most of the wall above it. They were exclusively theatrical photographs, and of a variety to suit all tastes. For the earnest student of the drama there was Sir Henry Irving in *The Bells*, and Mr Martin Harvey in *The Only Way*. For the admirers of the merely beautiful there were Messrs Dan Leno and Herbert Campbell.

'Not bad,' said Trevor. 'Beastly waste of money.'

'Waste of money!' Milton was surprised and pained at the criticism. 'Why, you must spend your money on *something*.'

'Rot, I call it,' said Trevor. 'If you want to collect something, why don't you collect something worth having?'

Just then Renford came back with the supplies.

'Thanks,' said Milton, 'put 'em down. Does the billy boil, young Renford?'

Renford asked for explanatory notes.

'You're a bit of an ass at times, aren't you?' said Milton, kindly. 'What I meant was, is the tea ready? If it is, you can scoot. If it isn't, buck up with it.'

A sound of bubbling and a rush of steam from the spout of the kettle proclaimed that the billy did boil. Renford extinguished the Etna, and left the room, while Milton, murmuring vague formulae about 'one spoonful for each person and one for the pot', got out of his chair with a groan – for the Town match had been an energetic one – and began to prepare tea.

'What I really came round about—' began Trevor.

'Half a second. I can't find the milk.'

He went to the door, and shouted for Renford. On that overworked youth's appearance, the following dialogue took place.

'Where's the milk?'

'What milk?'

'My milk.'

'There isn't any.' This in a tone not untinged with triumph, as if the speaker realised that here was a distinct score to him.

'No milk?'

'No.'

'Why not?'

'You never had any.'

'Well, just cut across – no, half a second. What are you doing downstairs?'

'Having tea.'

'Then you've got milk.'

'Only a little.' This apprehensively.

'Bring it up. You can have what we leave.'

Disgusted retirement of Master Renford.

'What I really came about,' said Trevor again, 'was business.'

'Colours?' inquired Milton, rummaging in the tin for biscuits with sugar on them. 'Good brand of biscuit you keep, Trevor.'

'Yes. I think we might give Alexander and Parker their third.'

'All right. Any others?'

'Barry his second, do you think?'

'Rather. He played a good game today. He's an improvement on Rand-Brown.'

'Glad you think so. I was wondering whether it was the right thing to do, chucking Rand-Brown out after one trial like that. But still, if you think Barry's better—'

'Streets better. I've had heaps of chances of watching them and comparing them, when they've been playing for the house. It isn't only that Rand-Brown can't tackle, and Barry can. Barry takes his passes much better, and doesn't lose his head when he's pressed.'

'Just what I thought,' said Trevor. 'Then you'd go on playing him for the first?'

'Rather. He'll get better every game, you'll see, as he gets more used to playing in the first three-quarter line. And he's as keen as anything on getting into the team. Practises taking passes and that sort of thing every day.'

'Well, he'll get his colours if we lick Ripton.'

'We ought to lick them. They've lost one of their forwards, Clifford, a red-haired chap, who was good out of touch. I don't know if you remember him.'

'I suppose I ought to go and see Allardyce about these colours, now. Goodbye.'

There was running and passing on the Monday for every one in the three teams. Trevor and Clowes met Mr Seymour as they were returning. Mr Seymour was the football master at Wrykyn.

'I see you've given Barry his second, Trevor.'

'Yes, sir.'

'I think you're wise to play him for the first. He knows the game, which is the great thing, and he will improve with practice,' said Mr Seymour, thus corroborating Milton's words of the previous Saturday.

'I'm glad Seymour thinks Barry good,' said Trevor, as they walked on. 'I shall go on playing him now.'

'Found out who wrote that letter yet?'

Trevor laughed.

'Not yet,' he said.

'Probably Rand-Brown,' suggested Clowes. 'He's the man who would gain most by Barry's not playing. I hear he had a row with Mill just before his study was ragged.'

'Everybody in Seymour's has had rows with Mill some time or other,' said Trevor.

Clowes stopped at the door of the junior day-room to find his fag. Trevor went on upstairs. In the passage he met Ruthven.

Ruthven seemed excited.

'I say, Trevor,' he exclaimed, 'have you seen your study?'

'Why, what's the matter with it?'

'You'd better go and look.'

Trevor went and looked.

It was rather an interesting sight. An earthquake or a cyclone might have made it a little more picturesque, but not much more. The general effect was not unlike that of an American saloon, after a visit from Mrs Carrie Nation (with hatchet). As in the case of Mill's study, the only thing that did not seem to have suffered any great damage was the table. Everything else looked rather off colour. The mantelpiece had been swept as bare as a bone, and its contents littered the floor. Trevor dived among the débris and retrieved the latest addition to his art gallery, the photograph of this year's first fifteen. It was a wreck. The glass was broken and the photograph itself slashed with a knife till most of the faces were unrecognisable. He picked up another treasure, last year's first eleven. Smashed glass again. Faces cut about with a knife as before. His collection of snapshots was torn into a thousand fragments, though, as Mr Jerome said of the papier-maché trout, there may only have been nine hundred. He did not count them. His bookshelf was empty. The books had gone to swell the contents of the floor. There was a Shakespeare with its cover off. Pages twenty-two to thirty-one of *Vice Versâ* had parted from the parent establishment, and were lying by themselves near the door. *The Rogues' March* lay just beyond them, and the look of the cover suggested that somebody had either been biting it or jumping on it with heavy boots.

There was other damage. Over the mantelpiece in happier days had hung a dozen sea gulls' eggs, threaded on a string. The string was still there, as good as new, but of the eggs nothing was to be seen, save a fine parti-coloured powder – on the floor, like everything else in the study. And a good deal of ink had been upset in one place and another.

Trevor had been staring at the ruins for some time, when he looked up to see Clowes standing in the doorway.

'Hullo,' said Clowes, 'been tidying up?'

Trevor made a few hasty comments on the situation. Clowes listened approvingly.

'Don't you think,' he went on, eyeing the study with a critical air, 'that you've got too many things on the floor, and too few anywhere else? And I should move some of those books on to the shelf, if I were you.'

Trevor breathed very hard.

'I should like to find the chap who did this,' he said softly.

Clowes advanced into the room and proceeded to pick up various misplaced articles of furniture in a helpful way.

'I thought so,' he said presently, 'come and look here.'

Tied to a chair, exactly as it had been in the case of Mill, was a neat white card, and on it were the words, '*With the Compliments of the League*'.

'What are you going to do about this?' asked Clowes. 'Come into my room and talk it over.'

'I'll tidy this place up first,' said Trevor. He felt that the work would be a relief. 'I don't want people to see this. It mustn't get about. I'm not going to have my study turned into a sort of sideshow, like Mill's. You go and change. I shan't be long.'

'I will *never* desert Mr Micawber,' said Clowes. 'Friend, my place is by your side. Shut the door and let's get to work.'

Ten minutes later the room had resumed a more or less – though principally less – normal appearance. The books and chairs were back in their places. The ink was sopped up. The broken photographs were stacked in a neat pile in one corner, with a rug over them. The mantelpiece was still empty, but, as Clowes pointed out, it now merely looked as if Trevor had been pawning some of his household gods. There was no sign that a devastating secret society had raged through the study.

Then they adjourned to Clowes' study, where Trevor sank into Clowes' second-best chair – Clowes, by an adroit movement, having appropriated the best one – with a sigh of enjoyment. Running and passing, followed by the toil of furniture-shifting, had made him feel quite tired.

'It doesn't look so bad now,' he said, thinking of the room they had left. 'By the way, what did you do with that card?'

'Here it is. Want it?'

'You can keep it. I don't want it.'

'Thanks. If this sort of things goes on, I shall get quite a nice collection of these cards. Start an album some day.'

'You know,' said Trevor, 'this is getting serious.'

'It always does get serious when anything bad happens to one's self. It always strikes one as rather funny when things happen to other people. When Mill's study was wrecked, I bet you regarded it as an amusing and original "turn". What do you think of the present effort?'

'Who on earth can have done it?'

'The Pres—'

'Oh, dry up. Of course it was. But who the blazes is he?'

'Nay, children, you have me there,' quoted Clowes. 'I'll tell you one thing, though. You remember what I said about its probably being Rand-Brown. He can't have done this, that's certain, because he was out in the fields the whole time. Though I don't see who else could have anything to gain by Barry not getting his colours.'

'There's no reason to suspect him at all, as far as I can see. I don't know much about him, bar the fact that he can't play footer for nuts, but I've never heard anything against him. Have you?'

'I scarcely know him myself. He isn't liked in Seymour's, I believe.'

'Well, anyhow, this can't be his work.'

'That's what I said.'

'For all we know, the League may have got their knife into Barry for some reason. You said they used to get their knife into fellows in that way. Anyhow, I mean to find out who ragged my room.'

'It wouldn't be a bad idea,' said Clowes.

O'Hara came round to Donaldson's before morning school next day to tell Trevor that he had not yet succeeded in finding the lost bat. He found Trevor and Clowes in the former's den, trying to put a few finishing touches to the same.

'Hullo, an' what's up with your study?' he inquired. He was quick at noticing things. Trevor looked annoyed. Clowes asked the visitor if he did not think the study presented a neat and gentlemanly appearance.

'Where are all your photographs, Trevor?' persisted the descendant of Irish kings.

'It's no good trying to conceal anything from the bhoy,' said Clowes. 'Sit down, O'Hara – mind that chair; it's rather wobbly – and I will tell ye the story.'

'Can you keep a thing dark?' inquired Trevor.

O'Hara protested that tombs were not in it.

'Well, then, do you remember what happened to Mill's study? That's what's been going on here.'

O'Hara nearly fell off his chair with surprise. That some philanthropist should rag Mill's study was only to be expected. Mill was one of the worst. A worm without a saving grace. But Trevor! Captain of football! In the first eleven! The thing was unthinkable.

'But who—?' he began.

'That's just what I want to know,' said Trevor, shortly. He did not enjoy discussing the affair.

'How long have you been at Wrykyn, O'Hara?' said Clowes.

O'Hara made a rapid calculation. His fingers twiddled in the air as he worked out the problem.

'Six years,' he said at last, leaning back exhausted with brain work.

'Then you must remember the League?'

'Remember the League? Rather.'

'Well, it's been revived.'

O'Hara whistled.

'This'll liven the old place up,' he said. 'I've often thought of reviving it meself. An' so has Moriarty. If it's anything like the Old League, there's going to be a sort of Donnybrook before it's done with. I wonder who's running it this time.'

'We should like to know that. If you find out, you might tell us.'

'I will.'

'And don't tell anybody else,' said Trevor. 'This business has got to be kept quiet. Keep it dark about my study having been ragged.'

'I won't tell a soul.'

'Not even Moriarty.'

'Oh, hang it, man,' put in Clowes, 'you don't want to kill the poor bhoy, surely? You must let him tell one person.'

'All right,' said Trevor, 'you can tell Moriarty. But nobody else, mind.'

O'Hara promised that Moriarty should receive the news exclusively.

'But why did the League go for ye?'

'They happen to be down on me. It doesn't matter why. They are.'

'I see,' said O'Hara. 'Oh,' he added, 'about that bat. The search is being "vigorously prosecuted" – that's a newspaper quotation—'

'*Times*?' inquired Clowes.

'*Wrykyn Patriot*,' said O'Hara, pulling out a bundle of letters. He inspected each envelope in turn, and from the fifth extracted a newspaper cutting.

'Read that,' he said.

It was from the local paper, and ran as follows: –

'*Hooligan Outrage* – A painful sensation has been caused in the town by a deplorable ebullition of local Hooliganism, which has resulted in the wanton disfigurement of the splendid statue of Sir Eustace Briggs which stands in the New Recreation Grounds. Our readers will recollect that the statue was erected to commemorate the return of Sir Eustace as member for the borough of Wrykyn, by an overwhelming majority, at the last election. Last Tuesday some youths of the town, passing through the Recreation Grounds early in the morning, noticed that the face and body of the statue were completely covered with leaves and some black substance, which on examination proved to be tar. They speedily lodged information at the police station.

Everything seems to point to party spite as the motive for the outrage. In view of the forthcoming election, such an act is highly significant, and will serve sufficiently to indicate the tactics employed by our opponents. The search for the perpetrator (or perpetrators) of the dastardly act is being vigorously prosecuted, and we learn with satisfaction that the police have already several clues.'

'Clues!' said Clowes, handing back the paper, 'that means *the bat*. That gas about "our opponents" is all a blind to put you off your guard. You wait. There'll be more painful sensations before you've finished with this business.'

'They can't have found the bat, or why did they not say so?' observed O'Hara.

'Guile,' said Clowes, 'pure guile. If I were you, I should escape while I could. Try Callao. There's no extradition there.

> 'On no petition
> Is extradition
> Allowed in Callao.'

Either of you chaps coming over to school?'

Tuesday mornings at Wrykyn were devoted – up to the quarter to eleven interval – to the study of mathematics. That is to say, instead of going to their form-rooms, the various forms visited the out-of-the-way nooks and dens at the top of the buildings where the mathematical masters were wont to lurk, and spent a pleasant two hours there playing round games or reading fiction under the desk. Mathematics being one of the few branches of school learning which are of any use in after life, nobody ever dreamed of doing any work in that direction, least of all O'Hara. It was a theory of O'Hara's that he came to school to enjoy himself. To have done any work during a mathematics lessons would have struck him as a positive waste of time, especially as he was in Mr Banks' class. Mr Banks was a master who simply cried out to be ragged. Everything he did and said seemed to invite the members of his class to amuse themselves, and they amused themselves accordingly. One of the advantages of being under him was that it was possible to predict to a nicety the moment when one would be sent out of the room. This was found very convenient.

O'Hara's ally, Moriarty, was accustomed to take his mathematics with Mr Morgan, whose room was directly opposite Mr Banks'. With Mr Morgan it was not quite so easy to date one's expulsion from the room under ordinary circumstances, and in the normal wear and tear of the morning's work, but there was one particular action which could always be relied upon to produce the desired result. In one corner of the room stood a gigantic globe. The problem – how did it get into the room? – was one that had exercised the minds of many generations of Wrykinians. It was much too big to have come through the door. Some thought that the block had been built round it, others that it had been placed in the room in infancy, and had since grown. To refer the question to Mr Morgan would, in six cases out of ten, mean instant departure from the room. But to make the event certain, it was necessary to grasp the globe firmly and spin it round on its axis. That always proved successful. Mr Morgan would dash down from his dais, address the offender in spirited terms, and give him his marching orders at once and without further trouble.

Moriarty had arranged with O'Hara to set the globe rolling at ten sharp on this particular morning. O'Hara would then so arrange matters with Mr Banks that they could meet in the passage at that hour, when O'Hara wished to impart to his friend his information concerning the League.

O'Hara promised to be at the trysting-place at the hour mentioned.

He did not think there would be any difficulty about it. The news that the League had been revived meant that there would be trouble in the very near future, and the prospect of trouble was meat and drink to the Irishman in O'Hara. Consequently he felt in particularly good form for mathematics (as he interpreted the word). He thought that he would have no difficulty whatever in keeping Mr Banks bright and amused. The first step had to be to arouse in him an interest in life, to bring him into a frame of mind which would induce him to look severely rather than leniently on the next offender. This was effected as follows: –

It was Mr Banks' practice to set his class sums to work out, and, after some three-quarters of an hour had elapsed, to pass round the form what he called 'solutions'. These were large sheets of paper, on which he had worked out each sum in his neat handwriting to a happy ending. When the head of the form, to whom they were passed first, had finished with them, he would make a slight tear in one corner, and, having done so, hand them on to his neighbour. The neighbour, before giving them to *his* neighbour, would also tear them slightly. In time they would return to their patentee and proprietor, and it was then that things became exciting.

'Who tore these solutions like this?' asked Mr Banks, in the repressed voice of one who is determined that he *will* be calm.

No answer. The tattered solutions waved in the air.

He turned to Harringay, the head of the form.

'Harringay, did you tear these solutions like this?'

Indignant negative from Harringay. What he had done had been to make the small tear in the top left-hand corner. If Mr Banks had asked, 'Did you make this small tear in the top left-hand corner of these solutions?' Harringay would have scorned to deny the impeachment. But to claim the credit for the whole work would, he felt, be an act of flat dishonesty, and an injustice to his gifted *collaborateurs*.

'No, sir,' said Harringay.

'Browne!'

'Yes, sir?'

'Did you tear these solutions in this manner?'

'No, sir.'

And so on through the form.

Then Harringay rose after the manner of the debater who is conscious that he is going to say the popular thing.

'Sir—' he began.

'Sit down, Harringay.'

Harringay gracefully waved aside the absurd command.

'Sir,' he said, 'I think I am expressing the general consensus of opinion among my – ahem – fellow-students, when I say that this class sincerely regrets the unfortunate state the solutions have managed to get themselves into.'

'Hear, hear!' from a back bench.

'It is with—'

'Sit *down*, Harringay.'

'It is with heartfelt—'

'Harringay, if you do not sit down—'

'As your ludship pleases.' This *sotto voce*.

And Harringay resumed his seat amidst applause. O'Hara got up.

'As me frind who has just sat down was about to observe—'

'Sit *down*, O'Hara. The whole form will remain after the class.'

'—the unfortunate state the solutions have managed to get thimsilves into is sincerely regretted by this class. Sir, I think I am ixprissing the general consensus of opinion among my fellow-students whin I say that it is with heartfelt sorrow—'

'O'Hara!'

'Yes, sir?'

'Leave the room instantly.'

'Yes, sir.'

From the tower across the gravel came the melodious sound of chimes. The college clock was beginning to strike ten. He had scarcely got into the passage, and closed the door after him, when a roar as of a bereaved spirit rang through the room opposite, followed by a string of words, the only intelligible one being the noun-substantive 'globe', and the next moment the door opened and Moriarty came out. The last stroke of ten was just booming from the clock.

There was a large cupboard in the passage, the top of which made a very comfortable seat. They climbed on to this, and began to talk business.

'An' what was it ye wanted to tell me?' inquired Moriarty.

O'Hara related what he had learned from Trevor that morning.

'An' do ye know,' said Moriarty, when he had finished, 'I half suspected, when I heard that Mill's study had been ragged, that it might be the League that had done it. If ye remember, it was what they enjoyed doing, breaking up a man's happy home. They did it frequently.'

'But I can't understand them doing it to Trevor at all.'

'They'll do it to anybody they choose till they're caught at it.'

'If they are caught, there'll be a row.'

'We must catch 'em,' said Moriarty. Like O'Hara, he revelled in the prospect of a disturbance. O'Hara and he were going up to Aldershot at the end of the term, to try and bring back the light and middle-weight medals respectively. Moriarty had won the light-weight in the previous year, but, by reason of putting on a stone since the competition, was now no longer eligible for that class. O'Hara had not been up before, but the Wrykyn instructor, a good judge of pugilistic form, was of opinion that he ought to stand an excellent chance. As the prize-fighter in *Rodney Stone* says, 'When you get a good Irishman, you can't better 'em, but they're dreadful 'asty.' O'Hara was attending the gymnasium every night, in order to learn to curb his 'dreadful 'astiness', and acquire skill in its place.

'I wonder if Trevor would be any good in a row,' said Moriarty.

'He can't box,' said O'Hara, 'but he'd go on till he was killed entirely. I say, I'm getting rather tired of sitting here, aren't you? Let's go to the other end of the passage and have some cricket.'

So, having unearthed a piece of wood from the débris at the top of the cupboard, and rolled a handkerchief into a ball, they adjourned.

Recalling the stirring events of six years back, when the League had first been started, O'Hara remembered that the members of that enterprising society had been wont to hold meetings in a secluded spot, where it was unlikely that they would be disturbed. It seemed to him that the first thing he ought to do, if he wanted to make their nearer acquaintance now, was to find their present rendezvous. They must have one. They would never run the risk involved in holding mass-meetings in one another's studies. On the last occasion, it had been an old quarry away out on the downs. This had been proved by the not-to-be-shaken testimony of three school-house fags, who had wandered out one half-holiday with the unconcealed intention of finding the League's place of meeting. Unfortunately for them, they *had* found it. They were going down the path that led to the quarry before-mentioned, when they were unexpectedly seized, blindfolded, and carried off. An impromptu court-martial was held – in whispers – and the three explorers forth-with received the most spirited 'touching-up' they had ever experienced. Afterwards they were released, and returned to their house with their zeal for detection quite quenched. The episode had created a good deal of excitement in the school at the time.

On three successive afternoons, O'Hara and Moriarty scoured the downs, and on each occasion they drew blank. On the fourth day, just before lock-up, O'Hara, who had been to tea with

Gregson, of Day's, was going over to the gymnasium to keep a pugilistic appointment with Moriarty, when somebody ran swiftly past him in the direction of the boarding-houses. It was almost dark, for the days were still short, and he did not recognise the runner. But it puzzled him a little to think where he had sprung from. O'Hara was walking quite close to the wall of the College buildings, and the runner had passed between it and him. And he had not heard his footsteps. Then he understood, and his pulse quickened as he felt that he was on the track. Beneath the block was a large sort of cellar-basement. It was used as a store-room for chairs, and was never opened except when prize-day or some similar event occurred, when the chairs were needed. It was supposed to be locked at other times, but never was. The door was just by the spot where he was standing. As he stood there, half-a-dozen other vague forms dashed past him in a knot. One of them almost brushed against him. For a moment he thought of stopping him, but decided not to. He could wait.

On the following afternoon he slipped down into the basement soon after school. It was as black as pitch in the cellar. He took up a position near the door.

It seemed hours before anything happened. He was, indeed, almost giving up the thing as a bad job, when a ray of light cut through the blackness in front of him, and somebody slipped through the door. The next moment, a second form appeared dimly, and then the light was shut off again.

O'Hara could hear them groping their way past him. He waited no longer. It is difficult to tell where sound comes from in the dark. He plunged forward at a venture. His hand, swinging round in a semicircle, met something which felt like a shoulder. He slipped his grasp down to the arm, and clutched it with all the force at his disposal.

'Ow!' exclaimed the captive, with no uncertain voice. 'Let go, you ass, you're hurting.'

The voice was a treble voice. This surprised O'Hara. It looked very much as if he had put up the wrong bird. From the dimensions of the arm which he was holding, his prisoner seemed to be of tender years.

'Let go, Harvey, you idiot. I shall kick.'

Before the threat could be put into execution, O'Hara, who had been fumbling all this while in his pocket for a match, found one loose, and struck a light. The features of the owner of the arm – he was still holding it – were lit up for a moment.

'Why, it's young Renford!' he exclaimed. 'What are you doing down here?'

Renford, however, continued to pursue the topic of his arm, and the effect that the vice-like grip of the Irishman had had upon it.

'You've nearly broken it,' he said, complainingly.

'I'm sorry. I mistook you for somebody else. Who's that with you?'

'It's me,' said an ungrammatical voice.

'Who's me?'

'Harvey.'

At this point a soft yellow light lit up the more immediate neighbourhood. Harvey had brought a bicycle lamp into action.

'That's more like it,' said Renford. 'Look here, O'Hara, you won't split, will you?'

'I'm not an informer by profession, thanks,' said O'Hara.

'Oh, I know it's all right, really, but you can't be too careful, because one isn't allowed down here, and there'd be a beastly row if it got out about our being down here.'

'And *they* would be cobbed,' put in Harvey.

'Who are they?' asked O'Hara.

'Ferrets. Like to have a look at them?'

'*Ferrets!*'

'Yes. Harvey brought back a couple at the beginning of term. Ripping little beasts. We couldn't keep them in the house, as they'd have got dropped on in a second, so we had to think of somewhere else, and thought why not keep them down here?'

'Why, indeed?' said O'Hara. 'Do ye find they like it?'

'Oh, *they* don't mind,' said Harvey. 'We feed 'em twice a day. Once before breakfast – we take it in turns to get up early – and once directly after school. And on half-holidays and Sundays we take them out on to the downs.'

'What for?'

'Why, rabbits, of course. Renford brought back a saloon-pistol with him. We keep it locked up in a box – don't tell any one.'

'And what do ye do with the rabbits?'

'We pot at them as they come out of the holes.'

'Yes, but when ye hit 'em?'

'Oh,' said Renford, with some reluctance, 'we haven't exactly hit any yet.'

'We've got jolly near, though, lots of times,' said Harvey. 'Last Saturday I swear I wasn't more than a quarter of an inch off one of them. If it had been a decent-sized rabbit, I should have plugged it middle stump; only it was a small one, so I missed. But come and see them. We keep 'em right at the other end of the place, in case anybody comes in.'

'Have you ever seen anybody down here?' asked O'Hara.

'Once,' said Renford. 'Half-a-dozen chaps came down here once while we were feeding the ferrets. We waited till they'd got well in, then we nipped out quietly. They didn't see us.'

'Did you see who they were?'

'No. It was too dark. Here they are. Rummy old crib this, isn't it? Look out for your shins on the chairs. Switch on the light, Harvey. There, aren't they rippers? Quite tame, too. They know us quite well. They know they're going to be fed, too. Hullo, Sir Nigel! This is Sir Nigel. Out of the "White Company", you know. Don't let him nip your fingers. This other one's Sherlock Holmes.'

'Cats-s-s--s!!' said O'Hara. He had a sort of idea that that was the right thing to say to any animal that could chase and bite.

Renford was delighted to be able to show his ferrets off to so distinguished a visitor.

'What were you down here about?' inquired Harvey, when the little animals had had their meal, and had retired once more into private life.

O'Hara had expected this question, but he did not quite know what answer to give. Perhaps, on the whole, he thought, it would be best to tell them the real reason. If he refused to explain, their curiosity would be roused, which would be fatal. And to give any reason except the true one called for a display of impromptu invention of which he was not capable. Besides, they would not be likely to give away his secret while he held this one of theirs connected with the ferrets. He explained the situation briefly, and swore them to silence on the subject.

Renford's comment was brief.

'By Jove!' he observed.

Harvey went more deeply into the question.

'What makes you think they meet down here?' he asked.

'I saw some fellows cutting out of here last night. And you say ye've seen them here, too. I don't see what object they could have down here if they weren't the League holding a meeting. I don't see what else a chap would be after.'

'He might be keeping ferrets,' hazarded Renford.

'The whole school doesn't keep ferrets,' said O'Hara. 'You're unique in that way. No, it must be the League, an' I mean to wait here till they come.'

'Not all night?' asked Harvey. He had a great respect for O'Hara, whose reputation in the school for out-of-the-way doings was considerable. In the bright lexicon of O'Hara he believed there to be no such word as 'impossible'.

'No,' said O'Hara, 'but till lock-up. You two had better cut now.'

'Yes, I think we'd better,' said Harvey.

'And don't ye breathe a word about this to a soul' – a warning which extracted fervent promises of silence from both youths.

'This,' said Harvey, as they emerged on to the gravel, 'is something like. I'm jolly glad we're in it.'

'Rather. Do you think O'Hara will catch them?'

'He must if he waits down there long enough. They're certain to come again. Don't you wish you'd been here when the League was on before?'

'I should think I did. Race you over to the shop. I want to get something before it shuts.'

'Right ho!' And they disappeared.

\* \* \*

O'Hara waited where he was till six struck from the clock-tower, followed by the sound of the bell as it rang for lock-up. Then he picked his way carefully through the groves of chairs, barking his shins now and then on their out-turned legs, and, pushing open the door, went out into the open air. It felt very fresh and pleasant after the brand of atmosphere supplied in the vault. He then ran over to the gymnasium to meet Moriarty, feeling a little disgusted at the lack of success that had attended his detective efforts up to the present. So far he had nothing to show for his trouble except a good deal of dust on his clothes, and a dirty collar, but he was full of determination. He could play a waiting game.

It was a pity, as it happened, that O'Hara left the vault when he did. Five minutes after he had gone, six shadowy forms made their way silently and in single file through the doorway of the vault, which they closed carefully behind them. The fact that it was after lock-up was of small consequence. A good deal of latitude in that way was allowed at Wrykyn. It was the custom to go out, after the bell had sounded, to visit the gymnasium. In the winter and Easter terms, the gymnasium became a sort of social club. People went there with a very small intention of doing gymnastics. They went to lounge about, talking to cronies, in front of the two huge stoves which warmed the place. Occasionally, as a concession to the look of the thing, they would do an easy exercise or two on the horse or parallels, but, for the most part, they preferred the *rôle* of spectator. There was plenty to see. In one corner O'Hara and Moriarty would be sparring their nightly six rounds (in two batches of three rounds each). In another, Drummond, who was going up to Aldershot as a feather-weight, would be putting in a little practice with the instructor. On the apparatus, the members of the gymnastic six, including the two experts who were to carry the school colours to Aldershot in the spring, would be performing their usual marvels. It was worth dropping into the gymnasium of an evening. In no other place in the school were so many sights to be seen.

When you were surfeited with sightseeing, you went off to your house. And this was where the peculiar beauty of the gymnasium system came in. You went up to any master who happened to be there – there was always one at least – and observed in suave accents, 'Please, sir, can I have a paper?' Whereupon, he, taking a scrap of paper, would write upon it, 'J. O. Jones (or A. B. Smith or C. D. Robinson) left gymnasium at such-and-such a time'. And, by presenting this to the menial who opened the door to you at your house, you went in rejoicing, and all was peace.

Now, there was no mention on the paper of the hour at which you *came* to the gymnasium – only of the hour at which you left. Consequently, certain lawless spirits would range the neighbourhood after lock-up, and, by putting in a quarter of an hour at the gymnasium before returning to their houses, escape comment. To this class belonged the shadowy forms previously mentioned.

O'Hara had forgotten this custom, with the result that he was not at the vault when they arrived. Moriarty, to whom he confided between the rounds the substance of his evening's discoveries, reminded him of it.

'It's no good watching before lock-up,' he said. 'After six is the time they'll come, if they come at all.'

'Bedad, ye're right,' said O'Hara. 'One of these nights we'll take a night off from boxing, and go and watch.'

'Right,' said Moriarty. 'Are ye ready to go on?'

'Yes. I'm going to practise that left swing at the body this round. The one Fitzsimmons does.' And they 'put 'em up' once more.

On the evening following O'Hara's adventure in the vaults, Barry and M'Todd were in their study, getting out the tea-things. Most Wrykinians brewed in the winter and Easter terms, when the days were short and lock-up early. In the summer term there were other things to do – nets, which lasted till a quarter to seven (when lock-up was), and the baths – and brewing prac-tically ceased. But just now it was at its height, and every evening, at a quarter past five, there might be heard in the houses the sizzling of the succulent sausage and other rare delicacies. As a rule, one or two studies would club together to brew, instead of preparing solitary banquets. This was found both more convivial and more economical. At Seymour's, studies numbers five, six, and seven had always combined from time immemorial, and Barry, on obtaining study six, had carried on the tradition. In study five were Drummond and his friend De Bertini. In study seven, which was a smaller room and only capable of holding one person with any comfort, one James Rupert Leather-Twigg (that was his singular name, as Mr Gilbert has it) had taken up his abode. The name of Leather-Twigg having proved, at an early date in his career, too great a mouthful for Wrykyn, he was known to his friends and acquaintances by the euphonious title of Shoeblossom. The charm about the genial Shoeblossom was that you could never tell what he was going to do next. All that you could rely on with any certainty was that it would be something which would have been better left undone.

It was just five o'clock when Barry and M'Todd started to get things ready. They were not high enough up in the school to have fags, so that they had to do this for themselves.

Barry was still in football clothes. He had been out running and passing with the first fifteen. M'Todd, whose idea of exercise was winding up a watch, had been spending his time since school ceased in the study with a book. He was in his ordinary clothes. It was therefore fortunate that, when he upset the kettle (he nearly always did at some period of the evening's business), the contents spread themselves over Barry, and not over himself. Football clothes will stand any amount of water, whereas M'Todd's 'Youth's winter suiting at forty-two shillings and six-pence' might have been injured. Barry, however, did not look upon the episode in this philosophical light. He spoke to him eloquently for a while, and then sent him downstairs to fetch more water. While he was away, Drummond and De Bertini came in.

'Hullo,' said Drummond, 'tea ready?'

'Not much,' replied Barry, bitterly, 'not likely to be, either, at this rate. We'd just got the kettle going when that ass M'Todd plunged against the table and upset the lot over my bags. Lucky the beastly stuff wasn't boiling. I'm soaked.'

'While we wait – the sausages – Yes? – a good idea – M'Todd, he is downstairs – but to wait? No, no. Let us. Shall we? Is it not so? Yes?' observed Bertie, lucidly.

'Now construe,' said Barry, looking at the linguist with a bewildered expression. It was a source of no little inconvenience to his friends that De Bertini was so very fixed in his determination to speak English. He was a trier all the way, was De Bertini.

You rarely caught him helping out his remarks with the language of his native land. It was English or nothing with him. To most of his circle it might as well have been Zulu.

Drummond, either through natural genius or because he spent more time with him, was generally able to act as interpreter. Occasionally there would come a linguistic effort by which even he freely confessed himself baffled, and then they would pass on unsatisfied. But, as a rule, he was equal to the emergency. He was so now.

'What Bertie means,' he explained, 'is that it's no good us waiting for M'Todd to come back. He never could fill a kettle in less than ten minutes, and even then he's certain to spill it coming upstairs and have to go back again. Let's get on with the sausages.'

The pan had just been placed on the fire when M'Todd returned with the water. He tripped over the mat as he entered, and spilt about half a pint into one of his football boots, which stood inside the door, but the accident was comparatively trivial, and excited no remark.

'I wonder where that slacker Shoeblossom has got to,' said Barry. 'He never turns up in time to do any work. He seems to regard himself as a beastly guest. I wish we could finish the sausages before he comes. It would be a sell for him.'

'Not much chance of that,' said Drummond, who was kneeling before the fire and keeping an excited eye on the spluttering pan, '*you'll* see. He'll come just as we've finished cooking them. I believe the man waits outside with his ear to the keyhole. Hullo! Stand by with the plate. They'll be done in half a jiffy.'

Just as the last sausage was deposited in safety on the plate, the door opened, and Shoeblossom, looking as if he had not brushed his hair since early childhood, sidled in with an attempt at an easy nonchalance which was rendered quite impossible by the hopeless state of his conscience.

'Ah,' he said, 'brewing, I see. Can I be of any use?'

'We've finished years ago,' said Barry.

'Ages ago,' said M'Todd.

A look of intense alarm appeared on Shoeblossom's classical features.

'You've not finished, really?'

'We've finished cooking everything,' said Drummond. 'We haven't begun tea yet. Now, are you happy?'

Shoeblossom was. So happy that he felt he must do something to celebrate the occasion. He felt like a successful general. There must be *something* he could do to show that he regarded the situation with approval. He looked round the study. Ha! Happy thought – the frying-pan. That useful culinary instrument was lying in the fender, still bearing its cargo of fat, and beside it – a sight to stir the blood and make the heart beat faster – were the sausages, piled up on their plate.

Shoeblossom stooped. He seized the frying-pan. He gave it one twirl in the air. Then, before any one could stop him, he had turned it upside down over the fire. As has been already remarked, you could never predict exactly what James Rupert Leather-Twigg would be up to next.

When anything goes out of the frying-pan into the fire, it is usually productive of interesting by-products. The maxim applies to fat. The fat was in the fire with a vengeance. A great sheet of flame rushed out and up. Shoeblossom leaped back with a readiness highly creditable in one who was not a professional acrobat. The covering of the mantelpiece caught fire. The flames went roaring up the chimney.

Drummond, cool while everything else was so hot, without a

word moved to the mantelpiece to beat out the fire with a foot-ball shirt. Bertie was talking rapidly to himself in French. Nobody could understand what he was saying, which was possibly fortunate.

By the time Drummond had extinguished the mantelpiece, Barry had also done good work by knocking the fire into the grate with the poker. M'Todd, who had been standing up till now in the far corner of the room, gaping vaguely at things in general, now came into action. Probably it was force of habit that suggested to him that the time had come to upset the kettle. At any rate, upset it he did – most of it over the glowing, blazing mass in the grate, the rest over Barry. One of the largest and most detestable smells the study had ever had to endure instantly assailed their nostrils. The fire in the study was out now, but in the chimney it still blazed merrily.

'Go up on to the roof and heave water down,' said Drummond, the strategist. 'You can get out from Milton's dormitory window. And take care not to chuck it down the wrong chimney.'

Barry was starting for the door to carry out these excellent instructions, when it flew open.

'Pah! *What* have you boys been doing? What an abominable smell. Pah!' said a muffled voice. It was Mr Seymour. Most of his face was concealed in a large handkerchief, but by the look of his eyes, which appeared above, he did not seem pleased. He took in the situation at a glance. Fires in the house were not rarities. One facetious sportsman had once made a rule of setting the senior day-room chimney on fire every term. He had since left (by request), but fires still occurred.

'Is the chimney on fire?'

'Yes, sir,' said Drummond.

'Go and find Herbert, and tell him to take some water on to

the roof and throw it down.' Herbert was the boot and knife cleaner at Seymour's.

Barry went. Soon afterwards a splash of water in the grate announced that the intrepid Herbert was hard at it. Another followed, and another. Then there was a pause. Mr Seymour thought he would look up to see if the fire was out. He stooped and peered into the darkness, and, even as he gazed, splash came the contents of the fourth pail, together with some soot with which they had formed a travelling acquaintance on the way down. Mr Seymour staggered back, grimy and dripping. There was dead silence in the study. Shoeblossom's face might have been seen working convulsively.

The silence was broken by a hollow, sepulchral voice with a strong Cockney accent.

'Did yer see any water come down then, sir?' said the voice.

Shoeblossom collapsed into a chair, and began to sob feebly.

'—disgraceful ... scandalous ... get *up*, Leather-Twigg ... not to be trusted ... *babies* ... three hundred lines, Leather-Twigg ... abominable ... surprised ... ought to be ashamed of yourselves ... *double*, Leather-Twigg ... not fit to have studies ... atrocious ...—'

Such were the main heads of Mr Seymour's speech on the situation as he dabbed desperately at the soot on his face with his handkerchief. Shoeblossom stood and gurgled throughout. Not even the thought of six hundred lines could quench that dauntless spirit.

'Finally,' perorated Mr Seymour, as he was leaving the room, 'as you are evidently not to be trusted with rooms of your own, I forbid you to enter them till further notice. It is disgraceful that such a thing should happen. Do you hear, Barry? And you,

Drummond? You are not to enter your studies again till I give you leave. Move your books down to the senior day-room tonight.'

And Mr Seymour stalked off to clean himself.

'Anyhow,' said Shoeblossom, as his footsteps died away, 'we saved the sausages.'

It is this indomitable gift of looking on the bright side that makes us Englishmen what we are.

It was something of a consolation to Barry and his friends – at any rate, to Barry and Drummond – that directly after they had been evicted from their study, the house-matches began. Except for the Ripton match, the house-matches were the most important event of the Easter term. Even the sports at the beginning of April were productive of less excitement. There were twelve houses at Wrykyn, and they played on the 'knocking-out' system. To be beaten once meant that a house was no longer eligible for the competition. It could play 'friendlies' as much as it liked, but, play it never so wisely, it could not lift the cup. Thus it often happened that a weak house, by fluking a victory over a strong rival, found itself, much to its surprise, in the semi-final, or sometimes even in the final. This was rarer at football than at cricket, for at football the better team generally wins.

The favourites this year were Donaldson's, though some fancied Seymour's. Donaldson's had Trevor, whose leadership was worth almost more than his play. In no other house was training so rigid. You could tell a Donaldson's man, if he was in his house-team, at a glance. If you saw a man eating oatmeal biscuits in the shop, and eyeing wistfully the while the stacks of buns and pastry, you could put him down as a Donaldsonite without further evidence. The captains of the other houses used to prescribe a certain amount of self-abnegation in the matter of food, but Trevor left his men barely enough to support life – enough, that is, of the things that are really worth eating. The consequence was that Donaldson's would turn out for an important match all muscle and bone, and on such occasions it was bad for those of their opponents who had been taking life more easily. Besides Trevor they had Clowes, and had had bad luck in not having Paget. Had Paget stopped, no other house could have looked at them. But by his departure, the strength of the team had become more nearly on a level with that of Seymour's.

Some even thought that Seymour's were the stronger. Milton was as good a forward as the school possessed. Besides him there were Barry and Rand-Brown on the wings. Drummond was a useful half, and five of the pack had either first or second fifteen colours. It was a team that would take some beating.

Trevor came to that conclusion early. 'If we can beat Seymour's, we'll lift the cup,' he said to Clowes.

'We'll have to do all we know,' was Clowes' reply.

They were watching Seymour's pile up an immense score against a scratch team got up by one of the masters. The first round of the competition was over. Donaldson's had beaten Templar's, Seymour's the School House. Templar's were rather stronger than the School House, and Donaldson's had beaten them by a rather larger score than that which Seymour's had run up in their match. But neither Trevor nor Clowes was inclined to draw any augury from this. Seymour's had taken things easily after half-time; Donaldson's had kept going hard all through.

'That makes Rand-Brown's fourth try,' said Clowes, as the wing three-quarter of the second fifteen raced round and scored in the corner.

'Yes. This is the sort of game he's all right in. The man who's marking him is no good. Barry's scored twice, and both good tries, too.'

'Oh, there's no doubt which is the best man,' said Clowes. 'I only mentioned that it was Rand-Brown's fourth as an item of interest.'

The game continued. Barry scored a third try.

'We're drawn against Appleby's next round,' said Trevor. 'We can manage them all right.'

'When is it?'

'Next Thursday. Nomads' match on Saturday. Then Ripton, Saturday week.'

'Who've Seymour's drawn?'

'Day's. It'll be a good game, too. Seymour's ought to win, but they'll have to play their best. Day's have got some good men.'

'Fine scrum,' said Clowes.

'Yes. Quick in the open, too, which is always good business. I wish they'd beat Seymour's.'

'Oh, we ought to be all right, whichever wins.'

Appleby's did not offer any very serious resistance to the Donaldson attack. They were outplayed at every point of the game, and, before half-time, Donaldson's had scored their thirty points. It was a rule in all in-school matches – and a good rule, too – that, when one side led by thirty points, the match stopped. This prevented those massacres which do so much towards crushing all the football out of the members of the beaten team; and it kept the winning team from getting slack, by urging them on to score their thirty points before half-time. There were some houses – notoriously slack – which would go for a couple of seasons without ever playing the second half of a match.

Having polished off the men of Appleby's, the Donaldson team trooped off to the other game to see how Seymour's were getting on with Day's. It was evidently an exciting match. The first half had been played to the accompaniment of much shouting from the ropes. Though coming so early in the competition, it was really the semi-final, for whichever team won would be almost certain to get into the final. The school had turned up in large numbers to watch.

'Seymour's looking tired of life,' said Clowes. 'That would seem as if his fellows weren't doing well.'

'What's been happening here?' asked Trevor of an enthusiast in a Seymour's house cap whose face was crimson with yelling.

'One goal all,' replied the enthusiast huskily. 'Did you beat Appleby's?'

'Yes. Thirty points before half-time. Who's been doing the scoring here?'

'Milton got in for us. He barged through out of touch. We've been pressing the whole time. Barry got over once, but he was held up. Hullo, they're beginning again. Buck up, Sey-*mour's*.'

His voice cracking on the high note, he took an immense slab of vanilla chocolate as a remedy for hoarseness.

'Who scored for Day's?' asked Clowes.

'Strachan. Rand-Brown let him through from their twenty-five. You never saw anything so rotten as Rand-Brown. He doesn't take his passes, and Strachan gets past him every time.'

'Is Strachan playing on the wing?'

Strachan was the first fifteen full-back.

'Yes. They've put young Bassett back instead of him. Sey-*mour's*. Buck up, Seymour's. We-ell played! There, did you ever see anything like it?' he broke off disgustedly.

The Seymourite playing centre next to Rand-Brown had run through to the back and passed out to his wing, as a good centre should. It was a perfect pass, except that it came at his head instead of his chest. Nobody with any pretensions to decent play should have missed it. Rand-Brown, however, achieved that feat. The ball struck his hands and bounded forward. The referee blew his whistle for a scrum, and a certain try was lost.

From the scrum the Seymour's forwards broke away to the goal-line, where they were pulled up by Bassett. The next minute the defence had been pierced, and Drummond was lying on the ball a yard across the line. The enthusiast standing by Clowes expended the last relics of his voice in commemorating the fact that his side had the lead.

'Drummond'll be good next year,' said Trevor. And he made a mental note to tell Allardyce, who would succeed him in the command of the school football, to keep an eye on the player in question.

The triumph of the Seymourites was not long lived. Milton failed to convert Drummond's try. From the drop-out from the twenty-five line Barry got the ball, and punted into touch. The throw-out was not straight, and a scrum was formed. The ball came out to the Day's halves, and went across to Strachan. Rand-Brown hesitated, and then made a futile spring at the first fifteen man's neck. Strachan handed him off easily, and ran. The Seymour's full-back, who was a poor player, failed to get across in time. Strachan ran round behind the posts, the kick succeeded, and Day's now led by two points.

After this the game continued in Day's half. Five minutes before time was up, Drummond got the ball from a scrum nearly on the line, passed it to Barry on the wing instead of opening up the game by passing to his centres, and Barry slipped through in the corner. This put Seymour's just one point ahead, and there they stayed till the whistle blew for no-side.

Milton walked over to the boarding-houses with Clowes and

THE GOLD BAT

Trevor. He was full of the match, particularly of the iniquity of Rand-Brown.

'I slanged him on the field,' he said. 'It's a thing I don't often do, but what else *can* you do when a man plays like that? He lost us three certain tries.'

'When did you administer your rebuke?' inquired Clowes.

'When he had let Strachan through that second time, in the second half. I asked him why on earth he tried to play footer at all. I told him a good kiss-in-the-ring club was about his form. It was rather cheap, but I felt so frightfully sick about it. It's sickening to be let down like that when you've been pressing the whole time, and ought to be scoring every other minute.'

'What had he to say on the subject?' asked Clowes.

'Oh, he gassed a bit until I told him I'd kick him if he said another word. That shut him up.'

'You ought to have kicked him. You want all the kicking practice you can get. I never saw anything feebler than that shot of yours after Drummond's try.'

'I'd like to see *you* take a kick like that. It was nearly on the touch-line. Still, when we play you, we shan't need to convert any of our tries. We'll get our thirty points without that. Perhaps you'd like to scratch?'

'As a matter of fact,' said Clowes confidentially, 'I am going to score seven tries against you off my own bat. You'll be sorry you ever turned out when we've finished with you.'

Shoeblossom sat disconsolately on the table in the senior day-room. He was not happy in exile. Brewing in the senior day-room was a mere vulgar brawl, lacking all the refining influences of the study. You had to fight for a place at the fire, and when you had got it 'twas not always easy to keep it, and there was no privacy, and the fellows were always bear-fighting, so that it was impossible to read a book quietly for ten consecutive minutes without some ass heaving a cushion at you or turning out the gas. Altogether Shoeblossom yearned for the peace of his study, and wished earnestly that Mr Seymour would withdraw the order of banishment. It was the not being able to read that he objected to chiefly. In place of brewing, the ex-proprietors of studies five, six, and seven now made a practice of going to the school shop. It was more expensive and not nearly so comfortable – there is a romance about a study brew which you can never get anywhere else – but it served, and it was not on this score that he grumbled most. What he hated was having to live in a bear-garden. For Shoeblossom was a man of moods. Give him two or three congenial spirits to back him up, and he would lead the revels with the *abandon* of a Mr Bultitude (after his return to his original form). But he liked to choose his accomplices, and the gay sparks of the senior day-room did not appeal to him. They were not intellectual enough. In his lucid intervals, he was accustomed to be almost abnormally solemn and respectable. When not promoting some unholy rag, Shoeblossom resembled an elderly gentleman of studious habits. He liked to sit in a comfortable chair and read a book. It was the impossibility of doing this in the senior day-room that led him to try and think of some other haven where he might rest. Had it been summer, he would have taken some literature out on to the cricket-field or the downs, and put in a little steady reading there, with the aid of a bag of cherries. But with the thermometer low, that was impossible.

He felt very lonely and dismal. He was not a man with many friends. In fact, Barry and the other three were almost the only members of the house with whom he was on speaking-terms. And of these four he saw very little. Drummond and Barry were always out of doors or over at the gymnasium, and as for M'Todd and De Bertini, it was not worth while talking to the one, and impossible to talk to the other. No wonder Shoeblossom felt dull. Once Barry and Drummond had taken him over to the gymnasium with them, but this had bored him worse than ever. They had been hard at it all the time – for, unlike a good many of the school, they went to the gymnasium for business, not to lounge – and he had had to sit about watching them. And watching gymnastics was one of the things he most loathed. Since then he had refused to go.

That night matters came to a head. Just as he had settled down to read, somebody, in flinging a cushion across the room, brought down the gas apparatus with a run, and before light was once more restored it was tea-time. After that there was preparation, which lasted for two hours, and by the time he had to go to bed he had not been able to read a single page of the enthralling work with which he was at present occupied.

He had just got into bed when he was struck with a brilliant idea. Why waste the precious hours in sleep? What was that saying of somebody's, 'Five hours' for a wise man, six for somebody else – he forgot whom – eight for a fool, nine for an idiot,' or words to that effect? Five hours' sleep would mean that he need not go to bed till half-past two. In the meanwhile he could be finding out exactly what the hero *did* do when he found out (to his horror) that it was his cousin Jasper who had really killed the old gentleman in the wood. The only question was – how was he to do his reading? Prefects were allowed to work on after lights-out in their dormitories by the aid of a candle, but to the ordinary mortal this was forbidden.

Then he was struck with another brilliant idea. It is a curious thing about ideas. You do not get one for over a month, and then there comes a rush of them, all brilliant. Why, he thought, should he not go and read in his study with a dark lantern? He had a dark lantern. It was one of the things he had found lying about at home on the last day of the holidays, and had brought with him to school. It was his custom to go about the house just before the holidays ended, snapping up unconsidered trifles, which might or might not come in useful. This term he had brought back a curious metal vase (which looked Indian, but which had probably been made in Birmingham the year before last), two old coins (of no mortal use to anybody in the world, including himself), and the dark lantern. It was reposing now in the cupboard in his study nearest the window.

He had brought his book up with him on coming to bed, on the chance that he might have time to read a page or two if he woke up early. (He had always been doubtful about that man Jasper. For one thing, he had been seen pawning the old gentleman's watch on the afternoon of the murder, which was a suspicious circumstance, and then he was not a nice character at all, and just the sort of man who would be likely to murder old gentlemen in woods.) He waited till Mr Seymour had paid his nightly visit – he went the round of the dormitories at about eleven – and then he chuckled gently. If Mill, the dormitory prefect, was awake, the chuckle would make him speak, for Mill was of a suspicious nature, and believed that it was only his unintermitted vigilance which prevented the dormitory ragging all night.

Mill *was* awake.

'Be quiet, there,' he growled. 'Shut up that noise.'

Shoeblossom felt that the time was not yet ripe for his departure. Half an hour later he tried again. There was no rebuke. To make certain he emitted a second chuckle, replete with sinister meaning. A slight snore came from the direction of Mill's bed. Shoeblossom crept out of the room, and hurried to his study. The door was not locked, for Mr Seymour had relied on his commands being sufficient to keep the owner out of it. He slipped in, found and lit the dark lantern, and settled down to read. He read with feverish excitement. The thing was, you see, that though Claud Trevelyan (that was the hero) knew jolly well that it was Jasper who had done the murder, the police didn't, and, as he (Claud) was too noble to tell them, he had himself been arrested on suspicion. Shoeblossom was skimming through the pages with starting eyes, when suddenly his attention was taken from his book by a sound. It was a footstep. Somebody was coming down the passage, and under the door filtered a thin stream of light. To snap the dark slide over the lantern and dart to the door, so that if it opened he would be behind it, was with him, as Mr Claud Trevelyan might have remarked, the work of a moment. He heard the door of study number five flung open, and then the footsteps passed on, and stopped opposite his own den. The handle turned, and the light of a candle flashed into the room, to be extinguished instantly as the draught of the moving door caught it.

Shoeblossom heard his visitor utter an exclamation of annoyance, and fumble in his pocket for matches. He recognised the voice. It was Mr Seymour's. The fact was that Mr Seymour had had the same experience as General Stanley in *The Pirates of Penzance*:

> The man who finds his conscience ache,
>     No peace at all enjoys;
> And, as I lay in bed awake,
>     I thought I heard a noise.

Whether Mr Seymour's conscience ached or not, cannot, of course, be discovered. But he had certainly thought he heard a noise, and he had come to investigate.

The search for matches had so far proved fruitless. Shoeblossom stood and quaked behind the door. The reek of hot tin from the dark lantern grew worse momentarily. Mr Seymour sniffed several times, until Shoeblossom thought that he must be discovered. Then, to his immense relief, the master walked away. Shoeblossom's chance had come. Mr Seymour had probably gone to get some matches to relight his candle. It was far from likely that the episode was closed. He would be back again presently. If Shoeblossom was going to escape, he must do it now, so he waited till the footsteps had passed away, and then darted out in the direction of his dormitory.

As he was passing Milton's study, a white figure glided out of it. All that he had ever read or heard of spectres rushed into Shoeblossom's petrified brain. He wished he was safely in bed.

He wished he had never come out of it. He wished he had led a better and nobler life. He wished he had never been born.

The figure passed quite close to him as he stood glued against the wall, and he saw it disappear into the dormitory opposite his own, of which Rigby was prefect. He blushed hotly at the thought of the fright he had been in. It was only somebody playing the same game as himself.

He jumped into bed and lay down, having first plunged the lantern bodily into his jug to extinguish it. Its indignant hiss had scarcely died away when Mr Seymour appeared at the door. It had occurred to Mr Seymour that he had smelt something very much out of the ordinary in Shoeblossom's study, a smell uncommonly like that of hot tin. And a suspicion dawned on him that Shoeblossom had been in there with a dark lantern. He had come to the dormitory to confirm his suspicions. But a glance showed him how unjust they had been. There was Shoeblossom fast asleep. Mr Seymour therefore followed the excellent example of my Lord Tomnoddy on a celebrated occasion, and went off to bed.

It was the custom for the captain of football at Wrykyn to select and publish the team for the Ripton match a week before the day on which it was to be played. On the evening after the Nomads' match, Trevor was sitting in his study writing out the names, when there came a knock at the door, and his fag entered with a letter.

'This has just come, Trevor,' he said.

'All right. Put it down.'

The fag left the room. Trevor picked up the letter. The handwriting was strange to him. The words had been printed. Then it flashed upon him that he had received a letter once before addressed in the same way – the letter from the League about Barry. Was this, too, from that address? He opened it.

It was.

He read it, and gasped. The worst had happened. The gold bat was in the hands of the enemy.

'With reference to our last communication,' ran the letter – the writer evidently believed in the commercial style – 'it may interest you to know that the bat you lost by the statue on the night of the 26th of January has come into our possession. *We observe that Barry is still playing for the first fifteen.*'

'And will jolly well continue to,' muttered Trevor, crumpling the paper viciously into a ball.

He went on writing the names for the Ripton match. The last name on the list was Barry's.

Then he sat back in his chair, and began to wrestle with this new development. Barry must play. That was certain. All the bluff in the world was not going to keep him from playing the best man at his disposal in the Ripton match. He himself did not count. It was the school he had to think of. This being so, what was likely to happen? Though nothing was said on the point, he felt certain that if he persisted in ignoring the League, that bat would find its way somehow – by devious routes, possibly – to the headmaster or some one else in authority. And then there would be questions – awkward questions – and things would begin to come out. Then a fresh point struck him, which was, that whatever might happen would affect, not himself, but O'Hara. This made it rather more of a problem how to act. Personally, he was one of those dogged characters who can put up with almost anything themselves. If this had been his affair, he would have gone on his way without hesitating. Evidently the writer of the letter was under the impression that he had been the hero (or villain) of the statue escapade.

If everything came out it did not require any great effort of prophecy to predict what the result would be. O'Hara would go. Promptly. He would receive his marching orders within ten minutes of the discovery of what he had done. He would be expelled twice over, so to speak, once for breaking out at night – one of the most heinous offences in the school code – and once for tarring the statue. Anything that gave the school a bad name in the town was a crime in the eyes of the powers, and this was such a particularly flagrant case. Yes, there was no doubt of that. O'Hara would take the first train home without waiting to pack up. Trevor knew his people well, and he could imagine their feelings when the prodigal strolled into their midst – an old Wrykinian *malgré lui*. As the philosopher said of falling off a ladder, it is not the falling that matters: it is the sudden stopping at the other end. It is not the being expelled that is so peculiarly objectionable: it is the sudden homecoming. With this gloomy vision before him, Trevor almost wavered. But the thought that the selection of the team had nothing whatever to do with his personal feelings strengthened him. He was simply a machine, devised to select the fifteen best men in the school to meet Ripton. In his official capacity of football captain he was not supposed to have any feelings. However, he yielded in so far that he went to Clowes to ask his opinion.

Clowes, having heard everything and seen the letter, unhesitatingly voted for the right course. If fifty mad Irishmen were to be expelled, Barry must play against Ripton. He was the best man, and in he must go.

'That's what I thought,' said Trevor. 'It's bad for O'Hara, though.'

Clowes remarked somewhat tritely that business was business.

'Besides,' he went on, 'you're assuming that the thing this letter hints at will really come off. I don't think it will. A man would have to be such an awful blackguard to go as low as that. The least grain of decency in him would stop him. I can imagine a man threatening to do it as a piece of bluff – by the way, the letter doesn't actually say anything of the sort, though I suppose it hints at it – but I can't imagine anybody out of a melodrama doing it.'

'You can never tell,' said Trevor. He felt that this was but an outside chance. The forbearance of one's antagonist is but a poor thing to trust to at the best of times.

'Are you going to tell O'Hara?' asked Clowes.

'I don't see the good. Would you?'

'No. He can't do anything, and it would only give him a bad time. There are pleasanter things, I should think, than going on from day to day not knowing whether you're going to be sacked or not within the next twelve hours. Don't tell him.'

'I won't. And Barry plays against Ripton.'

'Certainly. He's the best man.'

'I'm going over to Seymour's now,' said Trevor, after a pause, 'to see Milton. We've drawn Seymour's in the next round of the house-matches. I suppose you knew. I want to get it over before the Ripton match, for several reasons. About half the fifteen are playing on one side or the other, and it'll give them a good chance of getting fit. Running and passing is all right, but a good, hard game's the thing for putting you into form. And then I was thinking that, as the side that loses, whichever it is—'

'Seymour's, of course.'

'Hope so. Well, they're bound to be a bit sick at losing, so they'll play up all the harder on Saturday to console themselves for losing the cup.'

'My word, what strategy!' said Clowes. 'You think of everything. When do you think of playing it, then?'

'Wednesday struck me as a good day. Don't you think so?'

'It would do splendidly. It'll be a good match. For all practical purposes, of course, it's the final. If we beat Seymour's, I don't think the others will trouble us much.'

There was just time to see Milton before lock-up. Trevor ran across to Seymour's, and went up to his study.

'Come in,' said Milton, in answer to his knock.

Trevor went in, and stood surprised at the difference in the look of the place since the last time he had visited it. The walls, once covered with photographs, were bare. Milton, seated before the fire, was ruefully contemplating what looked like a heap of waste cardboard.

Trevor recognised the symptoms. He had had experience.

'You don't mean to say they've been at you, too!' he cried.

Milton's normally cheerful face was thunderous and gloomy.

'Yes. I was thinking what I'd like to do to the man who ragged it.'

'It's the League again, I suppose?'

Milton looked surprised.

'*Again?*' he said, 'where did *you* hear of the League? This is the first time I've heard of its existence, whatever it is. What *is* the confounded thing, and why on earth have they played the fool here? What's the meaning of this bally rot?'

He exhibited one of the variety of cards of which Trevor had already seen two specimens. Trevor explained briefly the style and nature of the League, and mentioned that his study also had been wrecked.

'Your study? Why, what have they got against you?'

'I don't know,' said Trevor. Nothing was to be gained by speaking of the letters he had received.

'Did they cut up your photographs?'

'Every one.'

'I tell you what it is, Trevor, old chap,' said Milton, with great solemnity, 'there's a lunatic in the school. That's what I make of it. A lunatic whose form of madness is wrecking studies.'

'But the same chap couldn't have done yours and mine. It must have been a Donaldson's fellow who did mine, and one of your chaps who did yours and Mill's.'

'Mill's? By Jove, of course. I never thought of that. That was the League, too, I suppose?'

'Yes. One of those cards was tied to a chair, but Clowes took it away before anybody saw it.'

Milton returned to the details of the disaster.

'Was there any ink spilt in your room?'

'Pints,' said Trevor, shortly. The subject was painful.

'So there was here,' said Milton, mournfully. 'Gallons.'

There was silence for a while, each pondering over his wrongs.

'Gallons,' said Milton again. 'I was ass enough to keep a large pot full of it here, and they used it all, every drop. You never saw such a sight.'

Trevor said he had seen one similar spectacle.

'And my photographs! You remember those photographs I showed you? All ruined. Slit across with a knife. Some torn in half. I wish I knew who did that.'

Trevor said he wished so, too.

'There was one of Mrs Patrick Campbell,' Milton continued in heartrending tones, 'which was torn into sixteen pieces. I counted them. There they are on the mantelpiece. And there was one of Little Tich' (here he almost broke down), 'which was so covered with ink that for half an hour I couldn't recognise it. Fact.'

Trevor nodded sympathetically.

'Yes,' said Milton. 'Soaked.'

There was another silence. Trevor felt it would be almost an outrage to discuss so prosaic a topic as the date of a house-match with one so broken up. Yet time was flying, and lock-up was drawing near.

'Are you willing to play—' he began.

'I feel as if I could never play again,' interrupted Milton. 'You'd hardly believe the amount of blotting-paper I've used today. It must have been a lunatic, Dick, old man.'

When Milton called Trevor 'Dick', it was a sign that he was moved. When he called him 'Dick, old man', it gave evidence of an internal upheaval without parallel.

'Why, who else but a lunatic would get up in the night to wreck another chap's study? All this was done between eleven last night and seven this morning. I turned in at eleven, and when I came down here again at seven the place was a wreck. It must have been a lunatic.'

'How do you account for the printed card from the League?'

Milton murmured something about madmen's cunning and diverting suspicion, and relapsed into silence. Trevor seized the opportunity to make the proposal he had come to make, that Donaldson's *v.* Seymour's should be played on the following Wednesday.

Milton agreed listlessly.

'Just where you're standing,' he said, 'I found a photograph of Sir Henry Irving so slashed about that I thought at first it was Huntley Wright in *San Toy*.'

'Start at two-thirty sharp,' said Trevor.

'I had seventeen of Edna May,' continued the stricken Seymourite, monotonously. 'In various attitudes. All destroyed.'

'On the first fifteen ground, of course,' said Trevor. 'I'll get Aldridge to referee. That'll suit you, I suppose?'

'All right. Anything you like. Just by the fireplace I found the remains of Arthur Roberts in *H.M.S. Irresponsible*. And part of Seymour Hicks. Under the table—'

Trevor departed.

'Suppose,' said Shoeblossom to Barry, as they were walking over to school on the morning following the day on which Milton's study had passed through the hands of the League, 'suppose you thought somebody had done something, but you weren't quite certain who, but you knew it was some one, what would you do?'

'What on *earth* do you mean?' inquired Barry.

'I was trying to make an A.B. case of it,' explained Shoe-blossom.

'What's an A.B. case?'

'I don't know,' admitted Shoeblossom, frankly. 'But it comes in a book of Stevenson's. I think it must mean a sort of case where you call every one A. and B. and don't tell their names.'

'Well, go ahead.'

'It's about Milton's study.'

'What! what about it?'

'Well, you see, the night it was ragged I was sitting in my study with a dark lantern—'

'What!'

Shoeblossom proceeded to relate the moving narrative of his night-walking adventure. He dwelt movingly on his state of mind when standing behind the door, waiting for Mr Seymour to come in and find him. He related with appropriate force the hair-raising episode of the weird white figure. And then he came to the conclusions he had since drawn (in calmer moments) from that apparition's movements.

'You see,' he said, 'I saw it coming out of Milton's study, and that must have been about the time the study was ragged. And it went into Rigby's dorm. So it must have been a chap in that dorm. who did it.'

Shoeblossom was quite clever at rare intervals. Even Barry, whose belief in his sanity was of the smallest, was compelled to admit that here, at any rate, he was talking sense.

'What would you do?' asked Shoeblossom.

'Tell Milton, of course,' said Barry.

'But he'd give me beans for being out of the dorm. after lights-out.'

This was a distinct point to be considered. The attitude of Barry towards Milton was different from that of Shoeblossom. Barry regarded him – through having played with him in impor-tant matches – as a good sort of fellow who had always behaved decently to him. Leather-Twigg, on the other hand, looked on him with undisguised apprehension, as one in authority who would give him lines the first time he came into contact with him, and cane him if he ever did it again. He had a decided disinclination to see Milton on any pretext whatever.

'Suppose I tell him?' suggested Barry.

'You'll keep my name dark?' said Shoeblossom, alarmed.

Barry said he would make an A.B. case of it.

After school he went to Milton's study, and found him still brooding over its departed glories.

'I say, Milton, can I speak to you for a second?'

'Hullo, Barry. Come in.'

Barry came in.

'I had forty-three photographs,' began Milton, without pre-amble. 'All destroyed. And I've no money to buy any more. I had seventeen of Edna May.'

Barry, feeling that he was expected to say something, said, 'By Jove! Really?'

'In various position,' continued Milton. 'All ruined.'

'Not really?' said Barry.

'There was one of Little Tich—'

But Barry felt unequal to playing the part of chorus any longer. It was all very thrilling, but, if Milton was going to run through the entire list of his destroyed photographs, life would be too short for conversation on any other topic.

'I say, Milton,' he said, 'it was about that that I came. I'm sorry—'

Milton sat up.

'It wasn't you who did this, was it?'

'No, no,' said Barry, hastily.

'Oh, I thought from your saying you were sorry—'

'I was going to say I thought I could put you on the track of the chap who did do it—'

For the second time since the interview began, Milton sat up.

'Go on,' he said.

'—But I'm sorry I can't give you the name of the fellow who told me about it.'

'That doesn't matter,' said Milton. 'Tell me the name of the fellow who did it. That'll satisfy me.'

'I'm afraid I can't do that, either.'

'Have you any idea what you *can* do?' asked Milton, satirically.

'I can tell you something which may put you on the right track.'

'That'll do for a start. Well?'

'Well, the chap who told me – I'll call him A.; I'm going to make an A.B. case of it – was coming out of his study at about one o'clock in the morning—'

'What the deuce was he doing that for?'

'Because he wanted to go back to bed,' said Barry.

'About time, too. Well?'

'As he was going past your study, a white figure emerged—'

'I should strongly advise you, young Barry,' said Milton, gravely, 'not to try and rot me in any way. You're a jolly good wing three-quarter, but you shouldn't presume on it. I'd slay the Old Man himself if he rotted me about this business.'

Barry was quite pained at this sceptical attitude in one whom he was going out of his way to assist.

'I'm not rotting,' he protested. 'This is all quite true.'

'Well, go on. You were saying something about white figures emerging.'

'Not white figures. A white figure,' corrected Barry. 'It came out of your study—'

'—And vanished through the wall?'

'It went into Rigby's dorm.,' said Barry, sulkily. It was maddening to have an exclusive bit of news treated in this way.

'Did it, by Jove!' said Milton, interested at last. 'Are you sure the chap who told you wasn't pulling your leg? Who was it told you?'

'I promised him not to say.'

'Out with it, young Barry.'

'I won't,' said Barry.

'You aren't going to tell me?'

'No.'

Milton gave up the point with much cheerfulness. He liked Barry, and he realised that he had no right to try and make him break his promise.

'That's all right,' he said. 'Thanks very much, Barry. This may be useful.'

'I'd tell you his name if I hadn't promised, you know, Milton.'

'It doesn't matter,' said Milton. 'It's not important.'

'Oh, there was one thing I forgot. It was a biggish chap the fellow saw.'

'How big? My size?'

'Not quite so tall, I should think. He said he was about Seymour's size.'

'Thanks. That's worth knowing. Thanks very much, Barry.'

When his visitor had gone, Milton proceeded to unearth one of the printed lists of the house which were used for purposes of roll-call. He meant to find out who were in Rigby's dormitory. He put a tick against the names. There were eighteen of them. The next thing was to find out which of them was about the same height as Mr Seymour. It was a somewhat vague description, for the house-master stood about five feet nine or eight, and a good many of the dormitory were that height, or near it. At last, after much brain-work, he reduced the number of 'possibles' to seven. These seven were Rigby himself, Linton, Rand-Brown, Griffith, Hunt, Kershaw, and Chapple. Rigby might be scratched off the list at once. He was one of Milton's greatest friends. Exeunt also Griffith, Hunt, and Kershaw. They were mild youths, quite incapable of any deed of devilry. There remained, therefore, Chapple, Linton, and Rand-Brown. Chapple was a boy who was invariably late for breakfast. The inference was that he was not likely to forego his sleep for the purpose of wrecking studies. Chapple might disappear from the list. Now there were only Linton and Rand-Brown to be considered. His suspicions fell on Rand-Brown. Linton was the last person, he thought, to do such a low thing. He was a cheerful, rollicking individual, who was popular with every one and seemed to like every one. He was not an orderly member of the house, certainly, and on several occasions Milton had found it necessary to drop on him heavily for creating disturbances. But he was not the sort that bears malice. He took it all in the way of business, and came up smiling after it was over. No, everything pointed to Rand-Brown. He and Milton had never got on well together, and quite recently they had quarrelled openly over the former's play in the Day's match. Rand-Brown must be the man. But Milton was sensible enough to feel that so far he had no real evidence whatever. He must wait.

On the following afternoon Seymour's turned out to play Donaldson's.

The game, like most house-matches, was played with the utmost keenness. Both teams had good three-quarters, and they attacked in turn. Seymour's had the best of it forward, where Milton was playing a great game, but Trevor in the centre was the best outside on the field, and pulled up rush after rush. By half-time neither side had scored.

After half-time Seymour's, playing downhill, came away with a rush to the Donaldsonites' half, and Rand-Brown, with one of the few decent runs he had made in good class football that term, ran in on the left. Milton took the kick, but failed, and Seymour's led by three points. For the next twenty minutes nothing more was scored. Then, when five minutes more of play remained, Trevor gave Clowes an easy opening, and Clowes sprinted between the posts. The kick was an easy one, and what sporting reporters term 'the major points' were easily added.

When there are five more minutes to play in an important house-match, and one side has scored a goal and the other a try, play is apt to become spirited. Both teams were doing all they knew. The ball came out to Barry on the right. Barry's abilities as a three-quarter rested chiefly on the fact that he could dodge well. This eel-like attribute compensated for a certain lack of pace. He was past the Donaldson's three-quarters in an instant, and running for the line, with only the back to pass, and with Clowes in hot pursuit. Another wriggle took him past the back, but it also gave Clowes time to catch him up. Clowes was a far faster runner, and he got to him just as he reached the twenty-five line. They came down together with a crash, Clowes on top, and as they fell the whistle blew.

'No-side,' said Mr Aldridge, the master who was refereeing.

Clowes got up.

'All over,' he said. 'Jolly good game. Hullo, what's up?'

For Barry seemed to be in trouble.

'You might give us a hand up,' said the latter. 'I believe I've twisted my beastly ankle or something.'

'I say,' said Clowes, helping him up, 'I'm awfully sorry. Did I do it? How did it happen?'

Barry was engaged in making various attempts at standing on the injured leg. The process seemed to be painful.

'Shall I get a stretcher or anything? Can you walk?'

'If you'd help me over to the house, I could manage all right. What a beastly nuisance! It wasn't your fault a bit. Only you tackled me when I was just trying to swerve, and my ankle was all twisted.'

Drummond came up, carrying Barry's blazer and sweater.

'Hullo, Barry,' he said, 'what's up? You aren't crocked?'

'Something gone wrong with my ankle. That my blazer? Thanks. Coming over to the house? Clowes was just going to help me over.'

Clowes asked a Donaldson's junior, who was lurking near at hand, to fetch his blazer and carry it over to the house, and then made his way with Drummond and the disabled Barry to Seymour's. Having arrived at the senior day-room, they deposited the injured three-quarter in a chair, and sent M'Todd, who came in at the moment, to fetch the doctor.

Dr Oakes was a big man with a breezy manner, the sort of doctor who hits you with the force of a sledge-hammer in the small ribs, and asks you if you felt anything *then*. It was on this principle that he acted with regard to Barry's ankle. He seized it in both hands and gave it a wrench.

'Did that hurt?' he inquired anxiously.

Barry turned white, and replied that it did.

Dr Oakes nodded wisely.

'Ah! H'm! Just so. 'Myes. Ah.'

'Is it bad?' asked Drummond, awed by these mystic utterances.

'My dear boy,' replied the doctor, breezily, 'it is always bad when one twists one's ankle.'

'How long will it do me out of footer?' asked Barry.

'How long? How long? How long? Why, fortnight. Fortnight,' said the doctor.

'Then I shan't be able to play next Saturday?'

'Next Saturday? Next Saturday? My dear boy, if you can put your foot to the ground by next Saturday, you may take it as evidence that the age of miracles is not past. Next Saturday, indeed! Ha, ha.'

It was not altogether his fault that he treated the matter with such brutal levity. It was a long time since he had been at school, and he could not quite realise what it meant to Barry not to be able to play against Ripton. As for Barry, he felt that he had never loathed and detested any one so thoroughly as he loathed and detested Dr Oakes at that moment.

'I don't see where the joke comes in,' said Clowes, when he had gone. 'I bar that man.'

'He's a beast,' said Drummond. 'I can't understand why they let a tout like that be the school doctor.'

Barry said nothing. He was too sore for words.

What Dr Oakes said to his wife that evening was: 'Over at the school, my dear, this afternoon. This afternoon. Boy with a twisted ankle. Nice young fellow. Very much put out when I told him he could not play football for a fortnight. But I chaffed him, and cheered him up in no time. I cheered him up in no time, my dear.'

'I'm sure you did, dear,' said Mrs Oakes. Which shows how differently the same thing may strike different people. Barry certainly did not look as if he had been cheered up when Clowes left the study and went over to tell Trevor that he would have to find a substitute for his right wing three-quarter against Ripton.

Trevor had left the field without noticing Barry's accident, and he was tremendously pleased at the result of the game.

'Good man,' he said, when Clowes came in, 'you saved the match.'

'And lost the Ripton match probably,' said Clowes, gloomily.

'What do you mean?'

'That last time I brought down Barry I crocked him. He's in his study now with a sprained ankle. I've just come from there. Oakes has seen him, and says he mustn't play for a fortnight.'

'Great Scott!' said Trevor, blankly. 'What on earth shall we do?'

'Why not move Strachan up to the wing, and put somebody else back instead of him? Strachan is a good wing.'

Trevor shook his head.

'No. There's nobody good enough to play back for the first. We mustn't risk it.'

'Then I suppose it must be Rand-Brown?'

'I suppose so.'

'He may do better than we think. He played quite a decent game today. That try he got wasn't half a bad one.'

'He'd be all right if he didn't funk. But perhaps he wouldn't funk against Ripton. In a match like that anybody would play up. I'll ask Milton and Allardyce about it.'

'I shouldn't go to Milton today,' said Clowes. 'I fancy he'll want a night's rest before he's fit to talk to. He must be a bit sick about this match. I know he expected Seymour's to win.'

He went out, but came back almost immediately.

'I say,' he said, 'there's one thing that's just occurred to me. This'll please the League. I mean, this ankle business of Barry's.'

The same idea had struck Trevor. It was certainly a respite. But he regretted it for all that. What he wanted was to beat Ripton, and Barry's absence would weaken the team. However, it was good in its way, and cleared the atmosphere for the time. The League would hardly do anything with regard to the carrying out of their threat while Barry was on the sick-list.

Next day, having given him time to get over the bitterness of defeat in accordance with Clowes' thoughtful suggestion, Trevor called on Milton, and asked him what his opinion was on the subject of the inclusion of Rand-Brown in the first fifteen in place of Barry.

'He's the next best man,' he added, in defence of the proposal.

'I suppose so,' said Milton. 'He'd better play, I suppose. There's no one else.'

'Clowes thought it wouldn't be a bad idea to shove Strachan on the wing, and put somebody else back.'

'Who is there to put?'

'Jervis?'

'Not good enough. No, it's better to be weakish on the wing than at back. Besides, Rand-Brown may do all right. He played well against you.'

'Yes,' said Trevor. 'Study looks a bit better now,' he added, as he was going, having looked round the room. 'Still a bit bare, though.'

Milton sighed. 'It will never be what it was.'

'Forty-three theatrical photographs want some replacing, of course,' said Trevor. 'But it isn't bad, considering.'

'How's yours?'

'Oh, mine's all right, except for the absence of photographs.'

'I say, Trevor.'

'Yes?' said Trevor, stopping at the door. Milton's voice had taken on the tone of one who is about to disclose dreadful secrets.

'Would you like to know what I think?'

'What?'

'Why, I'm pretty nearly sure who it was that ragged my study.'

'By Jove! What have you done to him?'

'Nothing as yet. I'm not quite sure of my man.'

'Who is the man?'

'Rand-Brown.'

'By Jove! Clowes once said he thought Rand-Brown must be the President of the League. But then, I don't see how you can account for *my* study being wrecked. He was out on the field when it was done.'

'Why, the League, of course. You don't suppose he's the only man in it? There must be a lot of them.'

'But what makes you think it was Rand-Brown?'

Milton told him the story of Shoeblossom, as Barry had told it to him. The only difference was that Trevor listened without any of the scepticism which Milton had displayed on hearing it. He was getting excited. It all fitted in so neatly. If ever there was circumstantial evidence against a man, here it was against Rand-Brown. Take the two cases. Milton had quarrelled with him. Milton's study was wrecked 'with the compliments of the League'. Trevor had turned him out of the first fifteen. Trevor's study was wrecked 'with the compliments of the League'. As Clowes had pointed out, the man with the most obvious motive for not wishing Barry to play for the school was Rand-Brown. It seemed a true bill.

'I shouldn't wonder if you're right,' he said, 'but of course one can't do anything yet. You want a lot more evidence. Anyhow, we must play him against Ripton, I suppose. Which is his study? I'll go and tell him now.'

'Ten.'

Trevor knocked at the door of study ten. Rand-Brown was sitting over the fire, reading. He jumped up when he saw that it was Trevor who had come in, and to his visitor it seemed that his face wore a guilty look.

'What do you want?' said Rand-Brown.

It was not the politest way of welcoming a visitor. It increased Trevor's suspicions. The man was afraid. A great idea darted into his mind. Why not go straight to the point and have it out with him here and now? He had the League's letter about the bat in his pocket. He would confront him with it and insist on searching the study there and then. If Rand-Brown were really, as he suspected, the writer of the letter, the bat must be in this room somewhere. Search it now, and he would have no time to hide it. He pulled out the letter.

'I believe you wrote that,' he said.

Trevor was always direct.

Rand-Brown seemed to turn a little pale, but his voice when he replied was quite steady.

'That's a lie,' he said.

'Then, perhaps,' said Trevor, 'you wouldn't object to proving it.'

'How?'

'By letting me search your study?'

'You don't believe my word?'

'Why should I? You don't believe mine.'

Rand-Brown made no comment on this remark.

'Was that what you came here for?' he asked.

'No,' said Trevor; 'as a matter of fact, I came to tell you to turn out for running and passing with the first tomorrow afternoon. You're playing against Ripton on Saturday.'

Rand-Brown's attitude underwent a complete transformation at the news. He became friendliness itself.

'All right,' he said. 'I say, I'm sorry I said what I did about lying. I was rather sick that you should think I wrote that rot you showed me. I hope you don't mind.'

'Not a bit. Do you mind my searching your study?'

For a moment Rand-Brown looked vicious. Then he sat down with a laugh.

'Go on,' he said; 'I see you don't believe me. Here are the keys if you want them.'

Trevor thanked him, and took the keys. He opened every drawer and examined the writing-desk. The bat was in none of these places. He looked in the cupboards. No bat there.

'Like to take up the carpet?' inquired Rand-Brown.

'No, thanks.'

'Search me if you like. Shall I turn out my pockets?'

'Yes, please,' said Trevor, to his surprise. He had not expected to be taken literally.

Rand-Brown emptied them, but the bat was not there.

Trevor turned to go.

'You've not looked inside the legs of the chairs yet,' said Rand-Brown. 'They may be hollow. There's no knowing.'

'It doesn't matter, thanks,' said Trevor. 'Sorry for troubling you. Don't forget tomorrow afternoon.'

And he went, with the very unpleasant feeling that he had been badly scored off.

It was a curious thing in connection with the matches between Ripton and Wrykyn, that Ripton always seemed to be the bigger team. They always had a gigantic pack of forwards, who looked capable of shoving a hole through one of the pyramids. Possibly they looked bigger to the Wrykinians than they really were. Strangers always look big on the football field. When you have grown accustomed to a person's appearance, he does not look nearly so large. Milton, for instance, never struck anybody at Wrykyn as being particularly big for a school forward, and yet today he was the heaviest man on the field by a quarter of a stone. But, taken in the mass, the Ripton pack were far heavier than their rivals. There was a legend current among the lower forms at Wrykyn that fellows were allowed to stop on at Ripton till they were twenty-five, simply to play football. This is scarcely likely to have been based on fact. Few lower form legends are.

Jevons, the Ripton captain, through having played opposite Trevor for three seasons – he was the Ripton left centre-three-quarter – had come to be quite an intimate of his. Trevor had gone down with Milton and Allardyce to meet the team at the station, and conduct them up to the school.

'How have you been getting on since Christmas?' asked Jevons.

'Pretty well. We've lost Paget, I suppose you know?'

'That was the fast man on the wing, wasn't it?'

'Yes.'

'Well, we've lost a man, too.'

'Oh, yes, that red-haired forward. I remember him.'

'It ought to make us pretty even. What's the ground like?'

'Bit greasy, I should think. We had some rain late last night.'

The ground *was* a bit greasy. So was the ball. When Milton kicked off up the hill with what wind there was in his favour, the outsides of both teams found it difficult to hold the ball. Jevons caught it on his twenty-five line, and promptly handed it forward. The first scrum was formed in the heart of the enemy's country.

A deep, swelling roar from either touch-line greeted the school's advantage. A feature of a big match was always the shouting. It rarely ceased throughout the whole course of the game, the monotonous but impressive sound of five hundred voices all shouting the same word. It was worth hearing. Sometimes the evenness of the noise would change to an excited *crescendo* as a school three-quarter got off, or the school back pulled up the attack with a fine piece of defence. Sometimes the shouting would give place to clapping when the school was being pressed and somebody had found touch with a long kick. But mostly the man on the ropes roared steadily and without cessation, and with the full force of his lungs, the word *'Wrykyn!'*

The scrum was a long one. For two minutes the forwards heaved and strained, now one side, now the other, gaining a few inches. The Wrykyn pack were doing all they knew to heel, but their opponents' superior weight was telling. Ripton had got the ball, and were keeping it. Their game was to break through with it and rush. Then suddenly one of their forwards kicked it on, and just at that moment the opposition of the Wrykyn pack gave way, and the scrum broke up. The ball came out on the Wrykyn side, and Allardyce whipped it out to Deacon, who was playing half with him.

'Ball's out,' cried the Ripton half who was taking the scrum. 'Break up. It's out.'

And his colleague on the left darted across to stop Trevor, who had taken Deacon's pass, and was running through on the right.

Trevor ran splendidly. He was a three-quarter who took a lot of stopping when he once got away. Jevons and the Ripton half met him almost simultaneously, and each slackened his pace for the fraction of a second, to allow the other to tackle. As they hesitated, Trevor passed them. He had long ago learned that to go hard when you have once started is the thing that pays.

He could see that Rand-Brown was racing up for the pass, and, as he reached the back, he sent the ball to him, waist-high. Then the back got to him, and he came down with a thud, with a vision, seen from the corner of his eye, of the ball bounding forward out of the wing three-quarter's hands into touch. Rand-Brown had bungled the pass in the old familiar way, and lost a certain try.

The touch-judge ran up with his flag waving in the air, but the referee had other views.

'Knocked on inside,' he said; 'scrum here.'

'Here' was, Trevor saw with unspeakable disgust, some three yards from the goal-line. Rand-Brown had only had to take the pass, and he must have scored.

The Ripton forwards were beginning to find their feet better now, and they carried the scrum. A truculent-looking warrior in one of those ear-guards which are tied on by strings underneath the chin, and which add fifty per cent to the ferocity of a forward's appearance, broke away with the ball at his feet, and swept down the field with the rest of the pack at his heels. Trevor arrived too late to pull up the rush, which had gone straight down the right touch-line, and it was not till Strachan fell on the ball on the Wrykyn twenty-five line that the danger ceased to threaten.

Even now the school were in a bad way. The enemy were pressing keenly, and a real piece of combination among their three-quarters would only too probably end in a try. Fortunately for them, Allardyce and Deacon were a better pair of halves than the couple they were marking. Also, the Ripton forwards heeled slowly, and Allardyce had generally got his man safely buried in the mud before he could pass.

He was just getting round for the tenth time to bottle his opponent as before, when he slipped. When the ball came out he was on all fours, and the Ripton exponent, finding to his great satisfaction that he had not been tackled, whipped the ball out on the left, where a wing three-quarter hovered.

This was the man Rand-Brown was supposed to be marking, and once again did Barry's substitute prove of what stuff his tackling powers were made. After his customary moment of hesitation, he had at the Riptonian's neck. The Riptonian handed him off in a manner that recalled the palmy days of the old Prize Ring – handing off was always slightly vigorous in the Ripton *v.* Wrykyn match – and dashed over the line in the extreme corner.

There was anguish on the two touch-lines. Trevor looked savage, but made no comment. The team lined up in silence.

It takes a very good kick to convert a try from the touch-line. Jevons' kick was a long one, but it fell short. Ripton led by a try to nothing.

A few more scrums near the halfway line, and a fine attempt

at a dropped goal by the Ripton back, and it was half-time, with the score unaltered.

During the interval there were lemons. An excellent thing is your lemon at half-time. It cools the mouth, quenches the thirst, stimulates the desire to be at them again, and improves the play.

Possibly the Wrykyn team had been happier in their choice of lemons on this occasion, for no sooner had the game been restarted than Clowes ran the whole length of the field, dodged through the three-quarters, punted over the back's head, and scored a really brilliant try, of the sort that Paget had been fond of scoring in the previous term. The man on the touch-line brightened up wonderfully, and began to try and calculate the probable score by the end of the game, on the assumption that, as a try had been scored in the first two minutes, ten would be scored in the first twenty, and so on.

But the calculations were based on false premises. After Strachan had failed to convert, and the game had been resumed with the score at one try all, play settled down in the centre, and neither side could pierce the other's defence. Once Jevons got off for Ripton, but Trevor brought him down safely, and once Rand-Brown let his man through, as before, but Strachan was there to meet him, and the effort came to nothing. For Wrykyn, no one did much except tackle. The forwards were beaten by the heavier pack, and seldom let the ball out. Allardyce intercepted a pass when about ten minutes of play remained, and ran through to the back. But the back, who was a capable man and in his third season in the team, laid him low scientifically before he could reach the line.

Altogether it looked as if the match were going to end in a draw. The Wrykyn defence, with the exception of Rand-Brown, was too good to be penetrated, while the Ripton forwards, by always getting the ball in the scrums, kept them from attacking. It was about five minutes from the end of the game when the Ripton right centre-three-quarter, in trying to punt across to the wing, miskicked and sent the ball straight into the hands of Trevor's colleague in the centre. Before his man could get round to him he had slipped through, with Trevor backing him up. The back, as a good back should, seeing two men coming at him, went for the man with the ball. But by the time he had brought him down, the ball was no longer where it had originally been. Trevor had got it, and was running in between the posts.

This time Strachan put on the extra two points without difficulty.

Ripton played their hardest for the remaining minutes, but without result. The game ended with Wrykyn a goal and a try ahead – a goal and two tries to a try. For the second time in one season the Ripton match had ended in a victory – a thing it was very rarely in the habit of doing.

The senior day-room at Seymour's rejoiced considerably that night. The air was dark with flying cushions, and darker still, occasionally, when the usual humorist turned the gas out. Milton was out, for he had gone to the dinner which followed the Ripton match, and the man in command of the house in his absence was Mill. And the senior day-room had no respect whatever for Mill.

Barry joined in the revels as well as his ankle would let him, but he was not feeling happy. The disappointment of being out of the first still weighed on him.

At about eight, when things were beginning to grow really lively, and the noise seemed likely to crack the window at any moment, the door was flung open and Milton stalked in.

'What's all this row?' he inquired. 'Stop it at once.'

As a matter of fact, the row *had* stopped – directly he came in.

'Is Barry here?' he asked.

'Yes,' said that youth.

'Congratulate you on your first, Barry. We've just had a meeting and given you your colours. Trevor told me to tell you.'

For the next three seconds you could have heard a cannon-ball drop. And that was equivalent, in the senior day-room at Seymour's, to a dead silence. Barry stood in the middle of the room leaning on the stick on which he supported life, now that his ankle had been injured, and turned red and white in regular rotation, as the magnificence of the news came home to him.

Then the small voice of Linton was heard.

'That'll be six d. I'll trouble you for, young Sammy,' said Linton. For he had betted an even sixpence with Master Samuel Menzies that Barry would get his first fifteen cap this term, and Barry had got it.

A great shout went up from every corner of the room. Barry was one of the most popular members of the house, and every one had been sorry for him when his sprained ankle had apparently put him out of the running for the last cap.

'Good old Barry,' said Drummond, delightedly. Barry thanked him in a dazed way.

Every one crowded in to shake his hand. Barry thanked them all in a dazed way.

And then the senior day-room, in spite of the fact that Milton had returned, gave itself up to celebrating the occasion with one of the most deafening uproars that had ever been heard even in that factory of noise. A babel of voices discussed the match of the afternoon, each trying to outshout the other. In one corner Linton was beating wildly on a biscuit-tin with part of a broken chair. Shoeblossom was busy in the opposite corner executing an intricate step-dance on somebody else's box. M'Todd had got hold of the red-hot poker, and was burning his initials in huge letters on the seat of a chair. Every one, in short, was enjoying himself, and it was not until an advanced hour that comparative quiet was restored. It was a great evening for Barry, the best he had ever experienced.

Clowes did not learn the news till he saw it on the notice-board, on the following Monday. When he saw it he whistled softly.

'I see you've given Barry his first,' he said to Trevor, when they met. 'Rather sensational.'

'Milton and Allardyce both thought he deserved it. If he'd been playing instead of Rand-Brown, they wouldn't have scored at all probably, and we should have got one more try.'

'That's all right,' said Clowes. 'He deserves it right enough, and I'm jolly glad you've given it him. But things will begin to move now, don't you think? The League ought to have a word to say about the business. It'll be a facer for them.'

'Do you remember,' asked Trevor, 'saying that you thought it must be Rand-Brown who wrote those letters?'

'Yes. Well?'

'Well, Milton had an idea that it was Rand-Brown who ragged his study.'

'What made him think that?'

Trevor related the Shoeblossom incident.

Clowes became quite excited.

'Then Rand-Brown must be the man,' he said. 'Why don't you go and tackle him? Probably he's got the bat in his study.'

'It's not in his study,' said Trevor, 'because I looked everywhere for it, and got him to turn out his pockets, too. And yet I'll swear he knows something about it. One thing struck me as a bit suspicious. I went straight into his study and showed him that last letter – about the bat, you know, and accused him of writing it. Now, if he hadn't been in the business somehow, he wouldn't have understood what was meant by their saying "the bat you lost". It might have been an ordinary cricket-bat for all he knew. But he offered to let me search the study. It didn't strike me as rum till afterwards. Then it seemed fishy. What do you think?'

Clowes thought so too, but admitted that he did not see of what use the suspicion was going to be. Whether Rand-Brown knew anything about the affair or not, it was quite certain that the bat was not with him.

O'Hara, meanwhile, had decided that the time had come for him to resume his detective duties. Moriarty agreed with him, and they resolved that that night they would patronise the vault instead of the gymnasium, and take a holiday as far as their boxing was concerned. There was plenty of time before the Aldershot competition.

Lock-up was still at six, so at a quarter to that hour they slipped down into the vault, and took up their position.

A quarter of an hour passed. The lock-up bell sounded faintly. Moriarty began to grow tired.

'Is it worth it?' he said, 'an' wouldn't they have come before, if they meant to come?'

'We'll give them another quarter of an hour,' said O'Hara. 'After that—'

'Sh!' whispered Moriarty.

The door had opened. They could see a figure dimly outlined in the semi-darkness. Footsteps passed down into the vault, and there came a sound as if the unknown had cannoned into a chair, followed by a sharp intake of breath, expressive of pain. A scraping sound, and a flash of light, and part of the vault was lit by a candle. O'Hara caught a glimpse of the unknown's face as he rose from lighting the candle, but it was not enough to enable him to recognise him. The candle was standing on a chair, and the light it gave was too feeble to reach the face of any one not on a level with it.

The unknown began to drag chairs out into the neighbourhood of the light. O'Hara counted six.

The sixth chair had scarcely been placed in position when the door opened again. Six other figures appeared in the opening one after the other, and bolted into the vault like rabbits into a burrow. The last of them closed the door after them.

O'Hara nudged Moriarty, and Moriarty nudged O'Hara; but neither made a sound. They were not likely to be seen – the blackness of the vault was too Egyptian for that – but they were so near to the chairs that the least whisper must have been heard. Not a word had proceeded from the occupants of the chairs so far. If O'Hara's suspicion was correct, and this was really the League holding a meeting, their methods were more secret than those of any other secret society in existence. Even the Nihilists probably exchanged a few remarks from time to time, when they met together to plot. But these men of mystery never opened their lips. It puzzled O'Hara.

The light of the candle was obscured for a moment, and a sound of puffing came from the darkness.

O'Hara nudged Moriarty again.

'Smoking!' said the nudge.

Moriarty nudged O'Hara.

'Smoking it is!' was the meaning of the movement.

A strong smell of tobacco showed that the diagnosis had been a true one. Each of the figures in turn lit his pipe at the candle, and sat back, still in silence. It could not have been very pleasant, smoking in almost pitch darkness, but it was breaking rules, which was probably the main consideration that swayed the smokers. They puffed away steadily, till the two Irishmen were wrapped about in invisible clouds.

Then a strange thing happened. I know that I am infringing copyright in making that statement, but it so exactly suits the occurrence, that perhaps Mr Rider Haggard will not object. It *was* a strange thing that happened.

A rasping voice shattered the silence

'You boys down there,' said the voice, 'come here immediately. Come here, I say.'

It was the well-known voice of Mr Robert Dexter, O'Hara and Moriarty's beloved house-master.

The two Irishmen simultaneously clutched one another, each afraid that the other would think – from force of long habit – that the house-master was speaking to him. Both stood where they were. It was the men of mystery and tobacco that Dexter was after, they thought.

But they were wrong. What had brought Dexter to the vault was the fact that he had seen two boys, who looked uncommonly like O'Hara and Moriarty, go down the steps of the vault at a quarter to six. He had been doing his usual after-lock-up prowl on the junior gravel, to intercept stragglers, and he had been a witness – from a distance of fifty yards, in a very bad light – of the descent into the vault. He had remained on the gravel ever since, in the hope of catching them as they came up; but as they had not come up, he had determined to make the first move himself. He had not seen the six unknowns go down, for, the evening being chilly, he had paced up and down, and they had by a lucky accident chosen a moment when his back was turned.

'Come up immediately,' he repeated.

Here a blast of tobacco-smoke rushed at him from the darkness. The candle had been extinguished at the first alarm, and he had not realised – though he had suspected it – that smoking had been going on.

A hurried whispering was in progress among the unknowns. Apparently they saw that the game was up, for they picked their way towards the door.

As each came up the steps and passed him, Mr Dexter observed 'Ha!' and appeared to make a note of his name. The last of the six was just leaving him after this process had been completed, when Mr Dexter called him back.

'That is not all,' he said, suspiciously.

'Yes, sir,' said the last of the unknowns.

Neither of the Irishmen recognised the voice. Its owner was a stranger to them.

'I tell you it is not,' snapped Mr Dexter. 'You are concealing the truth from me. O'Hara and Moriarty are down there – two boys in my own house. I saw them go down there.'

'They had nothing to do with us, sir. We saw nothing of them.'

'I have no doubt,' said the house-master, 'that you imagine that you are doing a very chivalrous thing by trying to hide them, but you will gain nothing by it. You may go.'

He came to the top of the steps, and it seemed as if he intended to plunge into the darkness in search of the suspects. But, probably realising the futility of such a course, he changed his mind, and delivered an ultimatum from the top step.

'O'Hara and Moriarty.'

No reply.

'O'Hara and Moriarty, I know perfectly well that you are down there. Come up immediately.'

Dignified silence from the vault.

'Well, I shall wait here till you do choose to come up. You would be well advised to do so immediately. I warn you, you will not tire me out.'

He turned, and the door slammed behind him.

'What'll we do?' whispered Moriarty. It was at last safe to whisper.

'Wait,' said O'Hara, 'I'm thinking.'

O'Hara thought. For many minutes he thought in vain. At last there came flooding back into his mind a memory of the days of his faghood. It was after that that he had been groping all the time. He remembered now. Once in those days there had been an unexpected function in the middle of term. There were needed for that function certain chairs. He could recall even now his furious disgust when he and a select body of fellow fags had been pounced upon by their form-master, and coerced into forming a line from the junior block to the cloisters, for the purpose of handing chairs. True, his form-master had stood ginger-beer after the event, with princely liberality, but the labour was of the sort that gallons of ginger-beer will not make pleasant. But he ceased to regret the episode now. He had been at the extreme end of the chair-handling chain. He had stood in a passage in the junior block, just by the door that led to the masters' garden, and which – he remembered – was never locked till late at night. And while he stood there, a pair of hands –

apparently without a body – had heaved up chair after chair through a black opening in the floor. In other words, a trap-door connected with the vault in which he now was.

He imparted these reminiscences of childhood to Moriarty. They set off to search for the missing door, and, after wanderings and barkings of shins too painful to relate, they found it. Moriarty lit a match. The light fell on the trap-door, and their last doubts were at an end. The thing opened inwards. The bolt was on their side, not in the passage above them. To shoot the bolt took them one second, to climb into the passage one minute. They stood at the side of the opening, and dusted their clothes.

'Bedad!' said Moriarty, suddenly.

'What?'

'Why, how are we to shut it?'

This was a problem that wanted some solving. Eventually they managed it, O'Hara leaning over and fishing for it, while Moriarty held his legs.

As luck would have it – and luck had stood by them well all through – there was a bolt on top of the trap-door, as well as beneath it.

'Supposing that had been shot!' said O'Hara, as they fastened the door in its place.

Moriarty did not care to suppose anything so unpleasant.

Mr Dexter was still prowling about on the junior gravel, when the two Irishmen ran round and across the senior gravel to the gymnasium. Here they put in a few minutes' gentle sparring, and then marched boldly up to Mr Day (who happened to have looked in five minutes after their arrival) and got their paper.

'What time did O'Hara and Moriarty arrive at the gymnasium?' asked Mr Dexter of Mr Day next morning.

'O'Hara and Moriarty? Really, I can't remember. I know they *left* at about a quarter to seven.'

That profound thinker, Mr Tony Weller, was never so correct as in his views respecting the value of an *alibi*. There are few better things in an emergency.

It was Renford's turn next morning to get up and feed the ferrets. Harvey had done it the day before.

Renford was not a youth who enjoyed early rising, but in the cause of the ferrets he would have endured anything, so at six punctually he slid out of bed, dressed quietly, so as not to disturb the rest of the dormitory, and ran over to the vault. To his utter amazement he found it locked. Such a thing had never been done before in the whole course of his experience. He tugged at the handle, but not an inch or a fraction of an inch would the door yield. The policy of the Open Door had ceased to find favour in the eyes of the authorities.

A feeling of blank despair seized upon him. He thought of the dismay of the ferrets when they woke up and realised that there was no chance of breakfast for them. And then they would gradually waste away, and some day somebody would go down to the vault to fetch chairs, and would come upon two mouldering skeletons, and wonder what they had once been. He almost wept at the vision so conjured up.

There was nobody about. Perhaps he might break in somehow. But then there was nothing to get to work with. He could not kick the door down. No, he must give it up, and the ferrets' breakfast-hour must be postponed. Possibly Harvey might be able to think of something.

'Fed 'em?' inquired Harvey, when they met at breakfast.

'No, I couldn't.'

'Why on earth not? You didn't oversleep yourself?'

Renford poured his tale into his friend's shocked ears.

'My hat!' said Harvey, when he had finished, 'what on earth are we to do? They'll starve.'

Renford nodded mournfully.

'Whatever made them go and lock the door?' he said.

He seemed to think the authorities should have given him due notice of such an action.

'You're sure they have locked it? It isn't only stuck or something?'

'I lugged at the handle for hours. But you can go and see for yourself if you like.'

Harvey went, and, waiting till the coast was clear, attached himself to the handle with a prehensile grasp, and put his back into one strenuous tug. It was even as Renford had said. The door was locked beyond possibility of doubt.

Renford and he went over to school that morning with long faces and a general air of acute depression. It was perhaps fortunate for their purpose that they did, for had their appearance been normal it might not have attracted O'Hara's attention. As it was, the Irishman, meeting them on the junior gravel, stopped and asked them what was wrong. Since the adventure in the vault, he had felt an interest in Renford and Harvey.

The two told their story in alternate sentences like the Strophe and Antistrophe of a Greek chorus. ('Steichomuthics', your Greek scholar calls it, I fancy. Ha, yes! Just so.)

'So ye can't get in because they've locked the door, an' ye don't know what to do about it?' said O'Hara, at the conclusion of the narrative.

Renford and Harvey informed him in chorus that that *was* the state of the game up to present date.

'An' ye want me to get them out for you?'

Neither had dared to hope that he would go so far as this. What they had looked for had been at the most a few thoughtful words of advice. That such a master-strategist as O'Hara should take up their cause was an unexampled piece of good luck.

'If you only would,' said Harvey.

'We should be most awfully obliged,' said Renford.

'Very well,' said O'Hara.

They thanked him profusely.

O'Hara replied that it would be a privilege.

He should be sorry, he said, to have anything happen to the ferrets.

Renford and Harvey went on into school feeling more cheerful. If the ferrets could be extracted from their present tight corner, O'Hara was the man to do it.

O'Hara had not made his offer of assistance in any spirit of doubt. He was certain that he could do what he had promised. For it had not escaped his memory that this was a Tuesday – in other words, a mathematics morning up to the quarter to eleven interval. That meant, as has been explained previously, that, while the rest of the school were in the form-rooms, he would be out in the passage, if he cared to be. There would be no witnesses to what he was going to do.

But, by that curious perversity of fate which is so often noticeable, Mr Banks was in a peculiarly lamb-like and long-suffering mood this morning. Actions for which O'Hara would on other days have been expelled from the room without hope of return, today were greeted with a mild 'Don't do that, please, O'Hara,' or even the ridiculously inadequate 'O'Hara!' It was perfectly disheartening. O'Hara began to ask himself bitterly what was the use of ragging at all if this was how it was received. And the moments were flying, and his promise to Renford and Harvey still remained unfulfilled.

He prepared for fresh efforts.

So desperate was he, that he even resorted to crude methods like the throwing of paper balls and the dropping of books. And when your really scientific ragger sinks to this, he is nearing the end of his tether. O'Hara hated to be rude, but there seemed no help for it.

The striking of a quarter past ten improved his chances. It had been privily agreed upon beforehand amongst the members of the class that at a quarter past ten every one was to sneeze simultaneously. The noise startled Mr Banks considerably. The angelic mood began to wear off. A man may be long-suffering, but he likes to draw the line somewhere.

'Another exhibition like that,' he said, sharply, 'and the class stays in after school, O'Hara!'

'Sir?'

'Silence.'

'I said nothing, sir, really.'

'Boy, you made a cat-like noise with your mouth.'

'What *sort* of noise, sir?'

The form waited breathlessly. This peculiarly insidious question had been invented for mathematical use by one Sandys, who had left at the end of the previous summer. It was but rarely that the master increased the gaiety of nations by answering the question in the manner desired.

Mr Banks, off his guard, fell into the trap.

'A noise like this,' he said curtly, and to the delighted audience came the melodious sound of a 'Mi-aou', which put O'Hara's effort completely in the shade, and would have challenged comparison with the war-cry of the stoutest mouser that ever trod a tile.

A storm of imitations arose from all parts of the room. Mr Banks turned pink, and, going straight to the root of the disturbance, forthwith evicted O'Hara.

O'Hara left with the satisfying feeling that his duty had been done.

Mr Banks' room was at the top of the middle block. He ran softly down the stairs at his best pace. It was not likely that the master would come out into the passage to see if he was still there, but it might happen, and it would be best to run as few risks as possible.

He sprinted over to the junior block, raised the trap-door, and jumped down. He knew where the ferrets had been placed, and had no difficulty in finding them. In another minute he was in the passage again, with the trap-door bolted behind him.

He now asked himself – what should he do with them? He must find a safe place, or his labours would have been in vain.

Behind the fives-court, he thought, would be the spot. Nobody ever went there. It meant a run of three hundred yards there and the same distance back, and there was more than a chance that he might be seen by one of the Powers. In which case he might find it rather hard to explain what he was doing in the middle of the grounds with a couple of ferrets in his possession when the hands of the clock pointed to twenty minutes to eleven.

But the odds were against his being seen. He risked it.

When the bell rang for the quarter to eleven interval the ferrets were in their new home, happily discussing a piece of meat – Renford's contribution, held over from the morning's meal, – and O'Hara, looking as if he had never left the passage for an instant, was making his way through the departing mathematical class to apologise handsomely to Mr Banks – as was his invariable custom – for his disgraceful behaviour during the morning's lesson.

School prefects at Wrykyn did weekly essays for the headmaster. Those who had got their scholarships at the 'Varsity, or who were going up in the following year, used to take their essays to him after school and read them to him – an unpopular and nerve-destroying practice, akin to suicide. Trevor had got his scholarship in the previous November. He was due at the headmaster's private house at six o'clock on the present Tuesday. He was looking forward to the ordeal not without apprehension. The essay subject this week had been 'One man's meat is another man's poison', and Clowes, whose idea of English Essay was that it should be a medium for intempestive frivolity, had insisted on his beginning with, 'While I cannot conscientiously go so far as to say that one man's meat is another man's poison, yet I am certainly of opinion that what is highly beneficial to one man may, on the other hand, to another man, differently constituted, be extremely deleterious, and, indeed, absolutely fatal.'

Trevor was not at all sure how the headmaster would take it. But Clowes had seemed so cut up at his suggestion that it had better be omitted, that he had allowed it to stand.

He was putting the final polish on this gem of English literature at half-past five, when Milton came in.

'Busy?' said Milton.

Trevor said he would be through in a minute.

Milton took a chair, and waited.

Trevor scratched out two words and substituted two others, made a couple of picturesque blots, and, laying down his pen, announced that he had finished.

'What's up?' he said.

'It's about the League,' said Milton.

'Found out anything?'

'Not anything much. But I've been making inquiries. You remember I asked you to let me look at those letters of yours?'

Trevor nodded. This had happened on the Sunday of that week.

'Well, I wanted to look at the post-marks.'

'By Jove, I never thought of that.'

Milton continued with the business-like air of the detective who explains in the last chapter of the book how he did it.

'I found, as I thought, that both letters came from the same place.'

Trevor pulled out the letters in question.

'So they do,' he said, 'Chesterton.'

'Do you know Chesterton?' asked Milton.

'Only by name.'

'It's a small hamlet about two miles from here across the downs. There's only one shop in the place, which acts as post-office and tobacconist and everything else. I thought that if I went there and asked about those letters, they might remember who it was that sent them, if I showed them a photograph.'

'By Jove,' said Trevor, 'of course! Did you? What happened?'

'I went there yesterday afternoon. I took about half-a-dozen photographs of various chaps, including Rand-Brown.'

'But wait a bit. If Chesterton's two miles off, Rand-Brown

couldn't have sent the letters. He wouldn't have the time after school. He was on the grounds both the afternoons before I got the letters.'

'I know,' said Milton; 'I didn't think of that at the time.'

'Well?'

'One of the points about the Chesterton post-office is that there's no letter-box outside. You have to go into the shop and hand anything you want to post across the counter. I thought this was a tremendous score for me. I thought they would be bound to remember who handed in the letters. There can't be many at a place like that.'

'Did they remember?'

'They remembered the letters being given in distinctly, but as for knowing anything beyond that, they were simply futile. There was an old woman in the shop, aged about three hundred and ten, I should think. I shouldn't say she had ever been very intelligent, but now she simply gibbered. I started off by laying out a shilling on some poisonous-looking sweets. I gave the lot to a village kid when I got out. I hope they didn't kill him. Then, having scattered ground-bait in that way, I lugged out the photographs, mentioned the letters and the date they had been sent, and asked her to weigh in and identify the sender.'

'Did she?'

'My dear chap, she identified them all, one after the other. The first was one of Clowes. She was prepared to swear on oath that that was the chap who had sent the letters. Then I shot a photograph of you across the counter, and doubts began to creep in. She said she was certain it was one of those two "la-ads", but couldn't quite say which. To keep her amused I fired in photograph number three – Allardyce's. She identified that, too. At the end of ten minutes she was pretty sure that it was one of the six

– the other three were Paget, Clephane, and Rand-Brown – but she was not going to bind herself down to any particular one. As I had come to the end of my stock of photographs, and was getting a bit sick of the game, I got up to go, when in came another ornament of Chesterton from a room at the back of the shop. He was quite a kid, not more than a hundred and fifty at the outside, so, as a last chance, I tackled him on the subject. He looked at the photographs for about half an hour, mumbling something about it not being "thiccy 'un" or "that 'un", or "that 'ere tother 'un", until I began to feel I'd had enough of it. Then it came out that the real chap who had sent the letters was a "la-ad" with light hair, not so big as me—'

'That doesn't help us much,' said Trevor.

'—And a "prarper little gennlemun". So all we've got to do is to look for some young duke of polished manners and exterior, with a thatch of light hair.'

'There are three hundred and sixty-seven fellows with light hair in the school,' said Trevor, calmly.

'Thought it was three hundred and sixty-eight myself,' said Milton, 'but I may be wrong. Anyhow, there you have the results of my investigations. If you can make anything out of them, you're welcome to it. Goodbye.'

'Half a second,' said Trevor, as he got up; 'had the fellow a cap of any sort?'

'No. Bareheaded. You wouldn't expect him to give himself away by wearing a house-cap?'

Trevor went over to the headmaster's revolving this discovery in his mind. It was not much of a clue, but the smallest clue is better than nothing. To find out that the sender of the League letters had fair hair narrowed the search down a little. It cleared the more raven-locked members of the school, at any rate.

Besides, by combining his information with Milton's, the search might be still further narrowed down. He knew that the polite letter-writer must be either in Seymour's or in Donaldson's. The number of fair-haired youths in the two houses was not excessive. Indeed, at the moment he could not recall any; which rather complicated matters.

He arrived at the headmaster's door, and knocked. He was shown into a room at the side of the hall, near the door. The butler informed him that the headmaster was engaged at present. Trevor, who knew the butler slightly through having constantly been to see the headmaster on business *via* the front door, asked who was there.

'Sir Eustace Briggs,' said the butler, and disappeared in the direction of his lair beyond the green baize partition at the end of the hall.

Trevor went into the room, which was a sort of spare study, and sat down, wondering what had brought the mayor of Wrykyn to see the headmaster at this advanced hour.

A quarter of an hour later the sound of voices broke in upon his peace. The headmaster was coming down the hall with the intention of showing his visitor out. The door of Trevor's room was ajar, and he could hear distinctly what was being said. He had no particular desire to play the eavesdropper, but the part was forced upon him.

Sir Eustace seemed excited.

'It is far from being my habit,' he was saying, 'to make unnecessary complaints respecting the conduct of the lads under your care.' (Sir Eustace Briggs had a distaste for the shorter and more colloquial forms of speech. He would have perished sooner than have substituted 'complain of your boys' for the majestic formula he had used. He spoke as if he enjoyed choosing his words. He seemed to pause and think before each word. Unkind people – who were jealous of his distinguished career – used to say that he did this because he was afraid of dropping an aitch if he relaxed his vigilance.)

'But,' continued he, 'I am reluctantly forced to the unpleasant conclusion that the dastardly outrage to which both I and the Press of the town have called your attention is to be attributed to one of the lads to whom I 'ave – *have* (this with a jerk) referred.'

'I will make a thorough inquiry, Sir Eustace,' said the bass voice of the headmaster.

'I thank you,' said the mayor. 'It would, under the circumstances, be nothing more, I think, than what is distinctly advisable. The man Samuel Wapshott, of whose narrative I have recently afforded you a brief synopsis, stated in no uncertain terms that he found at the foot of the statue on which the dastardly outrage was perpetrated a diminutive ornament, in shape like the bats that are used in the game of cricket. This ornament, he avers (with what truth I know not), was handed by him to a youth of an age coeval with that of the lads in the upper division of this school. The youth claimed it as his property, I was given to understand.'

'A thorough inquiry shall be made, Sir Eustace.'

'I thank you.'

And then the door shut, and the conversation ceased.

Trevor waited till the headmaster had gone back to his library, gave him five minutes to settle down, and then went in.

The headmaster looked up inquiringly.

'My essay, sir,' said Trevor.

'Ah, yes. I had forgotten.'

Trevor opened the notebook and began to read what he had written. He finished the paragraph which owed its insertion to Clowes, and raced hurriedly on to the next. To his surprise the flippancy passed unnoticed, at any rate, verbally. As a rule the headmaster preferred that quotations from back numbers of *Punch* should be kept out of the prefects' English Essays. And he generally said as much. But today he seemed strangely pre-occupied. A split infinitive in paragraph five, which at other times would have made him sit up in his chair stiff with horror, elicited no remark. The same immunity was accorded to the insertion (inspired by Clowes, as usual) of a popular catch phrase in the last few lines. Trevor finished with the feeling that luck had favoured him nobly.

'Yes,' said the headmaster, seemingly roused by the silence following on the conclusion of the essay. 'Yes.' Then, after a long pause, 'Yes,' again.

Trevor said nothing, but waited for further comment.

'Yes,' said the headmaster once more, 'I think that is a very fair essay. Very fair. It wants a little more – er – not quite so much – um – yes.'

Trevor made a note in his mind to effect these improvements in future essays, and was getting up, when the headmaster stopped him.

'Don't go, Trevor. I wish to speak to you.'

Trevor's first thought was, perhaps naturally, that the bat was going to be brought into discussion. He was wondering helplessly how he was going to keep O'Hara and his midnight exploit out of the conversation, when the headmaster resumed. 'An unpleasant thing has happened, Trevor—'

'Now we're coming to it,' thought Trevor.

'It appears, Trevor, that a considerable amount of smoking has been going on in the school.'

Trevor breathed freely once more. It was only going to be a mere conventional smoking row after all. He listened with more enjoyment as the headmaster, having stopped to turn down the wick of the reading-lamp which stood on the table at his side, and which had begun, appropriately enough, to smoke, resumed his discourse.

'Mr Dexter—'

Of course, thought Trevor. If there ever was a row in the school, Dexter was bound to be at the bottom of it.

'Mr Dexter has just been in to see me. He reported six boys. He discovered them in the vault beneath the junior block. Two of them were boys in your house.'

Trevor murmured something wordless, to show that the story interested him.

'You knew nothing of this, of course—'

'No, sir.'

'No. Of course not. It is difficult for the head of a house to know all that goes on in that house.'

Was this his beastly sarcasm? Trevor asked himself. But he came to the conclusion that it was not. After all, the head of a house is only human. He cannot be expected to keep an eye on the private life of every member of his house.

'This must be stopped, Trevor. There is no saying how widespread the practice has become or may become. What I want you to do is to go straight back to your house and begin a complete search of the studies.'

'Tonight, sir?' It seemed too late for such amusement.

'Tonight. But before you go to your house, call at Mr Seymour's, and tell Milton I should like to see him. And, Trevor.'

'Yes, sir?'

'You will understand that I am leaving this matter to you to be dealt with by you. I shall not require you to make any report to me. But if you should find tobacco in any boy's room, you must punish him well, Trevor. Punish him well.'

This meant that the culprit must be 'touched up' before the house assembled in the dining-room. Such an event did not often occur. The last occasion had been in Paget's first term as head of Donaldson's, when two of the senior day-room had been discovered attempting to revive the ancient and dishonourable custom of bullying. This time, Trevor foresaw, would set up a record in all probability. There might be any number of devotees of the weed, and he meant to carry out his instructions to the full, and make the criminals more unhappy than they had been since the day of their first cigar. Trevor hated the habit of smoking at school. He was so intensely keen on the success of the house and the school at games, that anything which tended to damage the wind and eye filled him with loathing. That anybody should dare to smoke in a house which was going to play in the final for the House Football Cup made him rage internally, and he proposed to make things bad and unrestful for such.

To smoke at school is to insult the divine weed. When you are obliged to smoke in odd corners, fearing every moment that you will be discovered, the whole meaning, poetry, romance of a pipe vanishes, and you become like those lost beings who smoke when they are running to catch trains. The boy who smokes at school is bound to come to a bad end. He will degenerate gradually into a person that plays dominoes in the smoking-rooms of A.B.C. shops with friends who wear bowler hats and frock coats.

Much of this philosophy Trevor expounded to Clowes in energetic language when he returned to Donaldson's after calling at Seymour's to deliver the message for Milton.

Clowes became quite animated at the prospect of a real row.

'We shall be able to see the skeletons in their cupboards,' he observed. 'Every man has a skeleton in his cupboard, which follows him about wherever he goes. Which study shall we go to first?'

'We?' said Trevor.

'We,' repeated Clowes firmly. 'I am not going to be left out of this jaunt. I need bracing up – I'm not strong, you know – and this is just the thing to do it. Besides, you'll want a bodyguard of some sort, in case the infuriated occupant turns and rends you.'

'I don't see what there is to enjoy in the business,' said Trevor, gloomily. 'Personally, I bar this kind of thing. By the time we've finished, there won't be a chap in the house I'm on speaking terms with.'

'Except me, dearest,' said Clowes. 'I will never desert you. It's of no use asking me, for I will never do it. Mr Micawber has his faults, but I will *never* desert Mr Micawber.'

'You can come if you like,' said Trevor; 'we'll take the studies in order. I suppose we needn't look up the prefects?'

'A prefect is above suspicion. Scratch the prefects.'

'That brings us to Dixon.'

Dixon was a stout youth with spectacles, who was popularly supposed to do twenty-two hours' work a day. It was believed that he put in two hours' sleep from eleven to one, and then got up and worked in his study till breakfast.

He was working when Clowes and Trevor came in. He dived head foremost into a huge Liddell and Scott as the door opened. On hearing Trevor's voice he slowly emerged, and a pair of round and spectacled eyes gazed blankly at the visitors. Trevor briefly explained his errand, but the interview lost in solemnity owing to the fact that the bare notion of Dixon storing tobacco in his room made Clowes roar with laughter. Also, Dixon stolidly refused to understand what Trevor was talking about, and at the end of ten minutes, finding it hopeless to try and explain, the two went. Dixon, with a hazy impression that he had been asked to join in some sort of round game, and had refused the offer, returned again to his Liddell and Scott, and continued to wrestle with the somewhat obscure utterances of the chorus in Æschylus' *Agamemnon*. The results of this fiasco on Trevor and Clowes were widely different. Trevor it depressed horribly. It made him feel savage. Clowes, on the other hand, regarded the whole affair in a spirit of rollicking farce, and refused to see that this was a serious matter, in which the honour of the house was involved.

The next study was Ruthven's. This fact somewhat toned down the exuberances of Clowes' demeanour. When one particularly dislikes a person, one has a curious objection to seeming in good spirits in his presence. One feels that he may take it as a sort of compliment to himself, or, at any rate, contribute grins of his own, which would be hateful. Clowes was as grave as Trevor when they entered the study.

Ruthven's study was like himself, overdressed and rather futile. It ran to little china ornaments in a good deal of profusion. It was more like a drawing-room than a school study.

'Sorry to disturb you, Ruthven,' said Trevor.

'Oh, come in,' said Ruthven, in a tired voice. 'Please shut the door; there is a draught. Do you want anything?'

'We've got to have a look round,' said Clowes.

'Can't you see everything there is?'

Ruthven hated Clowes as much as Clowes hated him.

Trevor cut into the conversation again.

'It's like this, Ruthven,' he said. 'I'm awfully sorry, but the Old Man's just told me to search the studies in case any of the fellows have got baccy.'

Ruthven jumped up, pale with consternation.

'You can't. I won't have you disturbing my study.'

'This is rot,' said Trevor, shortly, 'I've got to. It's no good making it more unpleasant for me than it is.'

'But I've no tobacco. I swear I haven't.'

'Then why mind us searching?' said Clowes affably.

'Come on, Ruthven,' said Trevor, 'chuck us over the keys. You might as well.'

'I won't.'

'Don't be an ass, man.'

'We have here,' observed Clowes, in his sad, solemn way, 'a stout and serviceable poker.' He stooped, as he spoke, to pick it up.

'Leave that poker alone,' cried Ruthven.

Clowes straightened himself.

'I'll swop it for your keys,' he said.

THE FINDING OF THE BAT

'Don't be a fool.'

'Very well, then. We will now crack our first crib.'

Ruthven sprang forward, but Clowes, handing him off in football fashion with his left hand, with his right dashed the poker against the lock of the drawer of the table by which he stood.

The lock broke with a sharp crack. It was not built with an eye to such onslaught.

'Neat for a first shot,' said Clowes, complacently. 'Now for the Umustaphas and shag.'

But as he looked into the drawer he uttered a sudden cry of excitement. He drew something out, and tossed it over to Trevor.

'Catch, Trevor,' he said quietly. 'Something that'll interest you.'

Trevor caught it neatly in one hand, and stood staring at it as if he had never seen anything like it before. And yet he had – often. For what he had caught was a little golden bat, about an inch long by an eighth of an inch wide.

'What do you think of that?' said Clowes.

Trevor said nothing. He could not quite grasp the situation. It was not only that he had got the idea so firmly into his head that it was Rand-Brown who had sent the letters and appropriated the bat. Even supposing he had not suspected Rand-Brown, he would never have dreamed of suspecting Ruthven. They had been friends. Not very close friends – Trevor's keenness for games and Ruthven's dislike of them prevented that – but a good deal more than acquaintances. He was so constituted that he could not grasp the frame of mind required for such an action as Ruthven's. It was something absolutely abnormal.

Clowes was equally surprised, but for a different reason. It was not so much the enormity of Ruthven's proceedings that took him aback. He believed him, with that cheerful intolerance which a certain type of mind affects, capable of anything. What surprised him was the fact that Ruthven had had the ingenuity and even the daring to conduct a campaign of this description. Cribbing in examinations he would have thought the limit of his crimes. Something backboneless and underhand of that kind would not have surprised him in the least. He would have said that it was just about what he had expected all along. But that

Ruthven should blossom out suddenly as quite an ingenious and capable criminal in this way, was a complete surprise.

'Well, perhaps *you'll* make a remark?' he said, turning to Ruthven.

Ruthven, looking very much like a passenger on a Channel steamer who has just discovered that the motion of the vessel is affecting him unpleasantly, had fallen into a chair when Clowes handed him off. He sat there with a look on his pasty face which was not good to see, as silent as Trevor. It seemed that whatever conversation there was going to be would have to take the form of a soliloquy from Clowes.

Clowes took a seat on the corner of the table.

'It seems to me, Ruthven,' he said, 'that you'd better say *something*. At present there's a lot that wants explaining. As this bat has been found lying in your drawer, I suppose we may take it that you're the impolite letter-writer?'

Ruthven found his voice at last.

'I'm not,' he cried; 'I never wrote a line.'

'Now we're getting at it,' said Clowes. 'I thought you couldn't have had it in you to carry this business through on your own. Apparently you've only been the sleeping partner in this show, though I suppose it was you who ragged Trevor's study? Not much sleeping about that. You took over the acting branch of the concern for that day only, I expect. Was it you who ragged the study?'

Ruthven stared into the fire, but said nothing.

'Must be polite, you know, Ruthven, and answer when you're spoken to. Was it you who ragged Trevor's study?'

'Yes,' said Ruthven.

'Thought so.'

'Why, of course, I met you just outside,' said Trevor, speaking for the first time. 'You were the chap who told me what had happened.'

Ruthven said nothing.

'The ragging of the study seems to have been all the active work he did,' remarked Clowes.

'No,' said Trevor, 'he posted the letters, whether he wrote them or not. Milton was telling me – you remember? I told you. No, I didn't. Milton found out that the letters were posted by a small, light-haired fellow.'

'That's him,' said Clowes, as regardless of grammar as the monks of Rheims, pointing with the poker at Ruthven's immaculate locks. 'Well, you ragged the study and posted the letters. That was all your share. Am I right in thinking Rand-Brown was the other partner?'

Silence from Ruthven.

'Am I?' persisted Clowes.

'You may think what you like. I don't care.'

'Now we're getting rude again,' complained Clowes. '*Was* Rand-Brown in this?'

'Yes,' said Ruthven.

'Thought so. And who else?'

'No one.'

'Try again.'

'I tell you there was no one else. Can't you believe a word a chap says?'

'A word here and there, perhaps,' said Clowes, as one making a concession, 'but not many, and this isn't one of them. Have another shot.'

Ruthven relapsed into silence.

'All right, then,' said Clowes, 'we'll accept that statement. There's just a chance that it may be true. And that's about all,

I think. This isn't my affair at all, really. It's yours, Trevor. I'm only a spectator and camp-follower. It's your business. You'll find me in my study.' And putting the poker carefully in its place, Clowes left the room. He went into his study, and tried to begin some work. But the beauties of the second book of Thucydides failed to appeal to him. His mind was elsewhere. He felt too excited with what had just happened to translate Greek. He pulled up a chair in front of the fire, and gave himself up to speculating how Trevor was getting on in the neighbouring study. He was glad he had left him to finish the business. If he had been in Trevor's place, there was nothing he would so greatly have disliked as to have some one – however familiar a friend – interfering in his wars and settling them for him. Left to himself, Clowes would probably have ended the interview by kicking Ruthven into the nearest approach to pulp compatible with the laws relating to manslaughter. He had an uneasy suspicion that Trevor would let him down far too easily.

The handle turned. Trevor came in, and pulled up another chair in silence. His face wore a look of disgust. But there were no signs of combat upon him. The toe of his boot was not worn and battered, as Clowes would have liked to have seen it. Evidently he had not chosen to adopt active and physical measures for the improvement of Ruthven's moral well-being.

'Well?' said Clowes.

'My word, what a hound!' breathed Trevor, half to himself.

'My sentiments to a hair,' said Clowes, approvingly. 'But what have you done?'

'I didn't do anything.'

'I was afraid you wouldn't. Did he give any explanation? What made him go in for the thing at all? What earthly motive could he have for not wanting Barry to get his colours, bar the fact that

Rand-Brown didn't want him to? And why should he do what Rand-Brown told him? I never even knew they were pals, before today.'

'He told me a good deal,' said Trevor. 'It's one of the beastliest things I ever heard. They neither of them come particularly well out of the business, but Rand-Brown comes worse out of it even than Ruthven. My word, that man wants killing.'

'That'll keep,' said Clowes, nodding. 'What's the yarn?'

'Do you remember about a year ago a chap named Patterson getting sacked?'

Clowes nodded again. He remembered the case well. Patterson had had gambling transactions with a Wrykyn tradesman, had been found out, and had gone.

'You remember what a surprise it was to everybody. It wasn't one of those cases where half the school suspects what's going on. Those cases always come out sooner or later. But Patterson nobody knew about.'

'Yes. Well?'

'Nobody,' said Trevor, 'except Ruthven, that is. Ruthven got to know somehow. I believe he was a bit of a pal of Patterson's at the time. Anyhow, – they had a row, and Ruthven went to Dexter – Patterson was in Dexter's – and sneaked. Dexter promised to keep his name out of the business, and went straight to the Old Man, and Patterson got turfed out on the spot. Then somehow or other Rand-Brown got to know about it – I believe Ruthven must have told him by accident some time or other. After that he simply had to do everything Rand-Brown wanted him to. Otherwise he said that he would tell the chaps about the Patterson affair. That put Ruthven in a dead funk.'

'Of course,' said Clowes; 'I should imagine friend Ruthven would have got rather a bad time of it. But what made them think of starting the League? It was a jolly smart idea. Rand-Brown's, of course?'

'Yes. I suppose he'd heard about it, and thought something might be made out of it if it were revived.'

'And were Ruthven and he the only two in it?'

'Ruthven swears they were, and I shouldn't wonder if he wasn't telling the truth, for once in his life. You see, everything the League's done so far could have been done by him and Rand-Brown, without anybody else's help. The only other studies that were ragged were Mill's and Milton's – both in Seymour's.'

'Yes,' said Clowes.

There was a pause. Clowes put another shovelful of coal on the fire.

'What are you going to do to Ruthven?'

'Nothing.'

'Nothing? Hang it, he doesn't deserve to get off like that. He isn't as bad as Rand-Brown – quite – but he's pretty nearly as finished a little beast as you could find.'

'Finished is just the word,' said Trevor. 'He's going at the end of the week.'

'Going? What! sacked?'

'Yes. The Old Man's been finding out things about him, apparently, and this smoking row has just added the finishing-touch to his discoveries. He's particularly keen against smoking just now for some reason.'

'But was Ruthven in it?'

'Yes. Didn't I tell you? He was one of the fellows Dexter caught in the vault. There were two in this house, you remember?'

'Who was the other?'

'That man Dashwood. Has the study next to Paget's old one. He's going, too.'

'Scarcely knew him. What sort of a chap was he?'

'Outsider. No good to the house in any way. He won't be missed.'

'And what are you going to do about Rand-Brown?'

'Fight him, of course. What else could I do?'

'But you're no match for him.'

'We'll see.'

'But you *aren't*,' persisted Clowes. 'He can give you a stone easily, and he's not a bad boxer either. Moriarty didn't beat him so very cheaply in the middle-weight this year. You wouldn't have a chance.'

Trevor flared up.

'Heavens, man,' he cried, 'do you think I don't know all that myself? But what on earth would you have me do? Besides, he may be a good boxer, but he's got no pluck at all. I might outstay him.'

'Hope so,' said Clowes.

But his tone was not hopeful.

Some people in Trevor's place might have taken the earliest opportunity of confronting Rand-Brown, so as to settle the matter in hand without delay. Trevor thought of doing this, but finally decided to let the matter rest for a day, until he should have found out with some accuracy what chance he stood.

After four o'clock, therefore, on the next day, having had tea in his study, he went across to the baths, in search of O'Hara. He intended that before the evening was over the Irishman should have imparted to him some of his skill with the hands. He did not know that for a man absolutely unscientific with his fists there is nothing so fatal as to take a boxing lesson on the eve of battle. A little knowledge is a dangerous thing. He is apt to lose his recklessness – which might have stood by him well – in exchange for a little quite useless science. He is neither one thing nor the other, neither a natural fighter nor a skilful boxer.

This point O'Hara endeavoured to press upon him as soon as he had explained why it was that he wanted coaching on this particular afternoon.

The Irishman was in the gymnasium, punching the ball, when Trevor found him. He generally put in a quarter of an hour with the punching-ball every evening, before Moriarty turned up for the customary six rounds.

'Want me to teach ye a few tricks?' he said. 'What's that for?'

'I've got a mill coming on soon,' explained Trevor, trying to make the statement as if it were the most ordinary thing in the world for a school prefect, who was also captain of football, head of a house, and in the cricket eleven, to be engaged for a fight in the near future.

'Mill!' exclaimed O'Hara. 'You! An' why?'

'Never mind why,' said Trevor. 'I'll tell you afterwards, perhaps. Shall I put on the gloves now?'

'Wait,' said O'Hara, 'I must do my quarter of an hour with the ball before I begin teaching other people how to box. Have ye a watch?'

'Yes.'

'Then time me. I'll do four rounds of three minutes each, with a minute's rest in between. That's more than I'll do at Aldershot, but it'll get me fit. Ready?'

'Time,' said Trevor.

He watched O'Hara assailing the swinging ball with considerable envy. Why, he wondered, had he not gone in for boxing? Everybody ought to learn to box. It was bound to come in useful some time or other. Take his own case. He was very much afraid – no, afraid was not the right word, for he was not that. He was very much of opinion that Rand-Brown was going to have a most enjoyable time when they met. And the final house-match was to be played next Monday. If events turned out as he could not help feeling they were likely to turn out, he would be too battered to play in that match. Donaldson's would probably win whether he played or not, but it would be bitter to be laid up on such an occasion. On the other hand, he must go through with it. He did not believe in letting other people take a hand in settling his private quarrels.

But he wished he had learned to box. If only he could hit that dancing, jumping ball with a fifth of the skill that O'Hara was displaying, his wiriness and pluck might see him through. O'Hara finished his fourth round with his leathern opponent, and sat down, panting.

'Pretty useful, that,' commented Trevor, admiringly.

'Ye should see Moriarty,' gasped O'Hara.

'Now, will ye tell me why it is you're going to fight, and with whom you're going to fight?'

'Very well. It's with Rand-Brown.'

'Rand-Brown!' exclaimed O'Hara. 'But, me dearr man, he'll ate you.'

Trevor gave a rather annoyed laugh. 'I must say I've got a nice, cheery, comforting lot of friends,' he said. 'That's just what Clowes has been trying to explain to me.'

'Clowes is quite right,' said O'Hara, seriously. 'Has the thing gone too far for ye to back out? Without climbing down, of course,' he added.

'Yes,' said Trevor, 'there's no question of my getting out of it. I daresay I could. In fact, I know I could. But I'm not going to.'

'But, me dearr man, ye haven't an earthly chance. I assure ye ye haven't. I've seen Rand-Brown with the gloves on. That was last term. He's not put them on since Moriarty bate him in the middles, so he may be out of practice. But even then he'd be a bad man to tackle. He's big an' he's strong, an' if he'd only had the heart in him he'd have been going up to Aldershot instead of Moriarty. That's what he'd be doing. An' you can't box at all. Never even had the gloves on.'

'Never. I used to scrap when I was a kid, though.'

'That's no use,' said O'Hara, decidedly. 'But you haven't said what it is that ye've got against Rand-Brown. What is it?'

THE GOLD BAT

'I don't see why I shouldn't tell you. You're in it as well. In fact, if it hadn't been for the bat turning up, you'd have been considerably more in it than I am.'

'What!' cried O'Hara. 'Where did you find it? Was it in the grounds? When was it you found it?'

Whereupon Trevor gave him a very full and exact account of what had happened. He showed him the two letters from the League, touched on Milton's connection with the affair, traced the gradual development of his suspicions, and described with some approach to excitement the scene in Ruthven's study, and the explanations that had followed it.

'Now do you wonder,' he concluded, 'that I feel as if a few rounds with Rand-Brown would do me good.'

O'Hara breathed hard.

'My word!' he said, 'I'd like to see ye kill him.'

'But,' said Trevor, 'as you and Clowes have been pointing out to me, if there's going to be a corpse, it'll be me. However, I mean to try. Now perhaps you wouldn't mind showing me a few tricks.'

'Take my advice,' said O'Hara, 'and don't try any of that foolery.'

'Why, I thought you were such a believer in science,' said Trevor in surprise.

'So I am, if you've enough of it. But it's the worst thing ye can do to learn a trick or two just before a fight, if you don't know anything about the game already. A tough, rushing fighter is ten times as good as a man who's just begun to learn what he oughtn't to do.'

'Well, what do you advise me to do, then?' asked Trevor, impressed by the unwonted earnestness with which the Irishman delivered this pugilistic homily, which was a paraphrase of the views dinned into the ears of every novice by the school instructor.

'I must do something.'

'The best thing ye can do,' said O'Hara, thinking for a moment, 'is to put on the gloves and have a round or two with me. Here's Moriarty at last. We'll get him to time us.'

As much explanation as was thought good for him having been given to the newcomer, to account for Trevor's newly-acquired taste for things pugilistic, Moriarty took the watch, with instructions to give them two minutes for the first round.

'Go as hard as you can,' said O'Hara to Trevor, as they faced one another, 'and hit as hard as you like. It won't be any practice if you don't. I sha'n't mind being hit. It'll do me good for Aldershot. See?'

Trevor said he saw.

'Time,' said Moriarty.

Trevor went in with a will. He was a little shy at first of putting all his weight into his blows. It was hard to forget that he felt friendly towards O'Hara. But he speedily awoke to the fact that the Irishman took his boxing very seriously, and was quite a different person when he had the gloves on. When he was so equipped, the man opposite him ceased to be either friend or foe in a private way. He was simply an opponent, and every time he hit him was one point. And, when he entered the ring, his only object in life for the next three minutes was to score points. Consequently Trevor, sparring lightly and in rather a futile manner at first, was woken up by a stinging flush hit between the eyes. After that he, too, forgot that he liked the man before him, and rushed him in all directions. There was no doubt as to who would have won if it had been a competition. Trevor's guard was of the most rudimentary order, and O'Hara got through when and how he liked. But though he took a good deal, he also gave a good deal, and O'Hara confessed himself not altogether sorry when Moriarty called 'Time'.

'Man,' he said regretfully, 'why ever did ye not take up boxing before? Ye'd have made a splendid middle-weight.'

'Well, have I a chance, do you think?' inquired Trevor.

'Ye might do it with luck,' said O'Hara, very doubtfully. 'But,' he added, 'I'm afraid ye've not much chance.'

And with this poor encouragement from his trainer and sparring-partner, Trevor was forced to be content.

The health of Master Harvey of Seymour's was so delicately constituted that it was an absolute necessity that he should consume one or more hot buns during the quarter of an hour's interval which split up morning school. He was tearing across the junior gravel towards the shop on the morning following Trevor's sparring practice with O'Hara, when a melodious treble voice called his name. It was Renford. He stopped, to allow his friend to come up with him, and then made as if to resume his way to the shop. But Renford proposed an amendment. 'Don't go to the shop,' he said, 'I want to talk.'

'Well, can't you talk in the shop?'

'Not what I want to tell you. It's private. Come for a stroll.'

Harvey hesitated. There were few things he enjoyed so much as exclusive items of school gossip (scandal preferably), but hot new buns were among those few things. However, he decided on this occasion to feed the mind at the expense of the body. He accepted Renford's invitation.

'What is it?' he asked, as they made for the football field. 'What's been happening?'

'It's frightfully exciting,' said Renford.

'What's up?'

'You mustn't tell any one.'

'All right. Of course not.'

'Well, then, there's been a big fight, and I'm one of the only chaps who know about it so far.'

'A fight?' Harvey became excited. 'Who between?'

Renford paused before delivering his news, to emphasise the importance of it.

'It was between O'Hara and Rand-Brown,' he said at length.

'*By Jove!*' said Harvey. Then a suspicion crept into his mind.

'Look here, Renford,' he said, 'if you're trying to green me—'

'I'm not, you ass,' replied Renford indignantly. 'It's perfectly true. I saw it myself.'

'By Jove, did you really? Where was it? When did it come off? Was it a good one? Who won?'

'It was the best one I've ever seen.'

'Did O'Hara beat him? I hope he did. O'Hara's a jolly good sort.'

'Yes. They had six rounds. Rand-Brown got knocked out in the middle of the sixth.'

'What, do you mean really knocked out, or did he just chuck it?'

'No. He was really knocked out. He was on the floor for quite a time. By Jove, you should have seen it. O'Hara was ripping in the sixth round. He was all over him.'

'Tell us about it,' said Harvey, and Renford told.

'I'd got up early,' he said, 'to feed the ferrets, and I was just cutting over to the fives-courts with their grub, when, just as I got across the senior gravel, I saw O'Hara and Moriarty standing waiting near the second court. O'Hara knows all about the ferrets, so I didn't try and cut or anything. I went up and began talking to him. I noticed he didn't look particularly keen on seeing me at first. I asked him if he was going to play fives. Then he said no, and told me what he'd really come for. He said he and Rand-Brown had had a row, and they'd agreed to have it out that morning in one of the fives-courts. Of course, when I heard that, I was all on to see it, so I said I'd wait, if he didn't mind. He said he didn't care, so long as I didn't tell everybody, so I said I wouldn't tell anybody except you, so he said all right, then, I could stop if I wanted to. So that was how I saw it. Well, after we'd been waiting a few minutes, Rand-Brown came in sight, with that beast Merrett in our house, who'd come to second him. It was just like one of those duels you read about, you know. Then O'Hara said that as I was the only one there with a watch – he and Rand-Brown were in footer clothes, and Merrett and Moriarty hadn't got their tickers on them – I'd better act as time-keeper. So I said all right, I would, and we went to the second fives-court. It's the biggest of them, you know. I stood outside on the bench, looking through the wire netting over the door, so as not to be in the way when they started scrapping. O'Hara and Rand-Brown took off their blazers and sweaters, and chucked them to Moriarty and Merrett, and then Moriarty and Merrett went and stood in two corners, and O'Hara and Rand-Brown walked into the middle and stood up to one another. Rand-Brown was miles the heaviest – by a stone, I should think – and he was taller and had a longer reach. But O'Hara looked much fitter. Rand-Brown looked rather flabby.

'I sang out "Time" through the wire netting, and they started off at once. O'Hara offered to shake hands, but Rand-Brown wouldn't. So they began without it.

'The first round was awfully fast. They kept having long rallies all over the place. O'Hara was a jolly sight quicker, and Rand-Brown didn't seem able to guard his hits at all. But he hit fright-fully hard himself, great, heavy slogs, and O'Hara kept getting them in the face. At last he got one bang in the mouth which knocked him down flat. He was up again in a second, and was starting to rush, when I looked at the watch, and found that I'd given them nearly half a minute too much already. So I shouted "Time", and made up my mind I'd keep more of an eye on the watch next round. I'd got so jolly excited, watching them, that I'd forgot I was supposed to be keeping time for them. They had only asked for a minute between the rounds, but as I'd given them half a minute too long in the first round, I chucked in a bit extra in the rest, so that they were both pretty fit by the time I started them again.

'The second round was just like the first, and so was the third. O'Hara kept getting the worst of it. He was knocked down three or four times more, and once, when he'd rushed Rand-Brown against one of the walls, he hit out and missed, and barked his knuckles jolly badly against the wall. That was in the middle of the third round, and Rand-Brown had it all his own way for the rest of the round – for about two minutes, that is to say. He hit O'Hara about all over the shop. I was so jolly keen on O'Hara's winning, that I had half a mind to call time early, so as to give him time to recover. But I thought it would be a low thing to do, so I gave them their full three minutes.

'Directly they began the fourth round, I noticed that things were going to change a bit. O'Hara had given up his rushing game, and was waiting for his man, and when he came at him he'd put in a hot counter, nearly always at the body. After a bit Rand-Brown began to get cautious, and wouldn't rush, so the fourth round was the quietest there had been. In the last minute they didn't hit each other at all. They simply sparred for openings. It was in the fifth round that O'Hara began to forge ahead. About half way through he got in a ripper, right in the wind, which almost doubled Rand-Brown up, and then he started rushing again. Rand-Brown looked awfully bad at the end of the round. Round six was ripping. I never saw two chaps go for each other so. It was one long rally. Then – how it happened I couldn't see, they were so quick – just as they had been at it a minute and a half, there was a crack, and the next thing I saw was Rand-Brown on the ground, looking beastly. He went down absolutely flat; his heels and head touched the ground at the same time.

'I counted ten out loud in the professional way like they do at the National Sporting Club, you know, and then said "O'Hara wins". I felt an awful swell. After about another half-minute, Rand-Brown was all right again, and he got up and went back to the house with Merrett, and O'Hara and Moriarty went off to Dexter's, and I gave the ferrets their grub, and cut back to breakfast.'

'Rand-Brown wasn't at breakfast,' said Harvey.

'No. He went to bed. I wonder what'll happen. Think there'll be a row about it?'

'Shouldn't think so,' said Harvey. 'They never do make rows about fights, and neither of them is a prefect, so I don't see what it matters if they *do* fight. But, I say—'

'What's up?'

'I wish,' said Harvey, his voice full of acute regret, 'that it had been my turn to feed those ferrets.'

'I don't,' said Renford cheerfully. 'I wouldn't have missed that mill for something. Hullo, there's the bell. We'd better run.'

When Trevor called at Seymour's that afternoon to see Rand-Brown, with a view to challenging him to deadly combat, and found that O'Hara had been before him, he ought to have felt relieved. His actual feeling was one of acute annoyance.

It seemed to him that O'Hara had exceeded the limits of friendship. It was all very well for him to take over the Rand-Brown contract, and settle it himself, in order to save Trevor from a very bad quarter of an hour, but Trevor was one of those people who object strongly to the interference of other people in their private business. He sought out O'Hara and complained. Within two minutes O'Hara's golden eloquence had soothed him and made him view the matter in quite a different light. What O'Hara pointed out was that it was not Trevor's affair at all, but his own. Who, he asked, had been likely to be damaged most by Rand-Brown's manoeuvres in connection with the lost bat? Trevor was bound to admit that O'Hara was that person. Very well, then, said O'Hara, then who had a better right to fight Rand-Brown? And Trevor confessed that no one else had a better.

'Then I suppose,' he said, 'that I shall have to do nothing about it?'

'That's it,' said O'Hara.

'It'll be rather beastly meeting the man after this,' said Trevor, presently. 'Do you think he might possibly leave at the end of term?'

'He's leaving at the end of the week,' said O'Hara. 'He was one of the fellows Dexter caught in the vault that evening. You won't see much more of Rand-Brown.'

'I'll try and put up with that,' said Trevor.

'And so will I,' replied O'Hara. 'And I shouldn't think Milton would be so very grieved.'

'No,' said Trevor. 'I tell you what will make him sick, though, and that is your having milled with Rand-Brown. It's a job he'd have liked to have taken on himself.'

Into the story at this point comes the narrative of Charles Mereweather Cook, aged fourteen, a day-boy.

Cook arrived at the school on the tenth of March, at precisely nine o'clock, in a state of excitement.

He said there was a row on in the town.

Cross-examined, he said there was no end of a row on in the town.

During morning school he explained further, whispering his tale into the attentive ear of Knight of the School House, who sat next to him.

What sort of a row, Knight wanted to know.

Cook deposed that he had been riding on his bicycle past the entrance to the Recreation Grounds on his way to school, when his eye was attracted by the movements of a mass of men just inside the gate. They appeared to be fighting. Witness did not stop to watch, much as he would have liked to do so. Why not? Why, because he was late already, and would have had to scorch anyhow, in order to get to school in time. And he had been late the day before, and was afraid that old Appleby (the master of the form) would give him beans if he were late again. Wherefore he had no notion of what the men were fighting about, but he betted that more would be heard about it. Why? Because, from what he saw of it, it seemed a jolly big thing. There must have been quite three hundred men fighting. (Knight, satirically, '*Pile* it on!') Well, quite a hundred, anyhow. Fifty a side. And fighting like anything. He betted there would be something about it in the *Wrykyn Patriot* tomorrow. He shouldn't wonder if somebody had been killed. What were they scrapping about? How should *he* know!

Here Mr Appleby, who had been trying for the last five minutes to find out where the whispering noise came from, at length traced it to its source, and forthwith requested Messrs Cook and Knight to do him two hundred lines, adding that, if he heard them talking again, he would put them into the extra lesson. Silence reigned from that moment.

Next day, while the form was wrestling with the moderately exciting account of Caesar's doings in Gaul, Master Cook produced from his pocket a newspaper cutting. This, having previously planted a forcible blow in his friend's ribs with an elbow to attract the latter's attention, he handed to Knight, and in dumb show requested him to peruse the same. Which Knight, feeling no interest whatever in Caesar's doings in Gaul, and having, in consequence, a good deal of time on his hands, proceeded to do. The cutting was headed 'Disgraceful Fracas', and was written in the elegant style that was always so marked a feature of the *Wrykyn Patriot*.

'We are sorry to have to report,' it ran, 'another of those deplorable ebullitions of local Hooliganism, to which it has before now been our painful duty to refer. Yesterday the Recreation Grounds were made the scene of as brutal an exhibition of savagery as has ever marred the fair fame of this town. Our

readers will remember how on a previous occasion, when the
fine statue of Sir Eustace Briggs was found covered with tar, we
attributed the act to the malevolence of the Radical section of the
community. Events have proved that we were right. Yesterday a
body of youths, belonging to the rival party, was discovered in
the very act of repeating the offence. A thick coating of tar had
already been administered, when several members of the rival
faction appeared. A free fight of a peculiarly violent nature
immediately ensued, with the result that, before the police could
interfere, several of the combatants had received severe bruises.
Fortunately the police then arrived on the scene, and with great
difficulty succeeded in putting a stop to the *fracas*. Several arrests
were made.

'We have no desire to discourage legitimate party rivalry, but
we feel justified in strongly protesting against such dastardly
tricks as those to which we have referred. We can assure our
opponents that they can gain nothing by such conduct.'

There was a good deal more to the effect that now was the
time for all good men to come to the aid of the party, and that
the constituents of Sir Eustace Briggs must look to it that they
failed not in the hour of need, and so on. That was what the
*Wrykyn Patriot* had to say on the subject.

O'Hara managed to get hold of a copy of the paper, and
showed it to Clowes and Trevor.

'So now,' he said, 'it's all right, ye see. They'll never suspect it
wasn't the same people that tarred the statue both times. An'
ye've got the bat back, so it's all right, ye see.'

'The only thing that'll trouble you now,' said Clowes, 'will be
your conscience.'

O'Hara intimated that he would try and put up with that.

'But isn't it a stroke of luck,' he said, 'that they should have gone and tarred Sir Eustace again so soon after Moriarty and I did it?'

Clowes said gravely that it only showed the force of good example.

'Yes. They wouldn't have thought of it, if it hadn't been for us,' chortled O'Hara. 'I wonder, now, if there's anything else we could do to that statue!' he added, meditatively.

'My good lunatic,' said Clowes, 'don't you think you've done almost enough for one term?'

'Well, 'myes,' replied O'Hara thoughtfully, 'perhaps we have, I suppose.'

The term wore on. Donaldson's won the final house-match by a matter of twenty-six points. It was, as they had expected, one of the easiest games they had had to play in the competition. Bryant's, who were their opponents, were not strong, and had only managed to get into the final owing to their luck in drawing weak opponents for the trial heats. The real final, that had decided the ownership of the cup, had been Donaldson's *v.* Seymour's.

Aldershot arrived, and the sports. Drummond and O'Hara covered themselves with glory, and brought home silver medals. But Moriarty, to the disappointment of the school, which had counted on his pulling off the middles, met a strenuous gentleman from St Paul's in the final, and was prematurely outed in the first minute of the third round. To him, therefore, there fell but a medal of bronze.

It was on the Sunday after the sports that Trevor's connection with the bat ceased – as far, that is to say, as concerned its unpleasant character (as a piece of evidence that might be used to his disadvantage). He had gone to supper with the headmaster, accompanied by Clowes and Milton. The headmaster nearly always invited a few of the house prefects to Sunday supper during the term. Sir Eustace Briggs happened to be there. He had withdrawn his insinuations concerning the part supposedly played by a member of the school in the matter of the tarred statue, and the headmaster had sealed the *entente cordiale* by asking him to supper.

An ordinary man might have considered it best to keep off the delicate subject. Not so Sir Eustace Briggs. He was on to it like glue. He talked of little else throughout the whole course of the meal.

'My suspicions,' he boomed, towards the conclusion of the feast, 'which have, I am rejoiced to say, proved so entirely void of foundation and significance, were aroused in the first instance, as I mentioned before, by the narrative of the man Samuel Wapshott.'

Nobody present showed the slightest desire to learn what the man Samuel Wapshott had had to say for himself, but Sir Eustace, undismayed, continued as if the whole table were hanging on his words.

'The man Samuel Wapshott,' he said, 'distinctly asserted that a small gold ornament, shaped like a bat, was handed by him to a lad of age coeval with these lads here.'

The headmaster interposed. He had evidently heard more than enough of the man Samuel Wapshott.

'He must have been mistaken,' he said briefly. 'The bat which Trevor is wearing on his watch-chain at this moment is the only one of its kind that I know of. You have never lost it, Trevor?'

Trevor thought for a moment. *He* had never lost it. He replied diplomatically, 'It has been in a drawer nearly all the term, sir,' he said.

'A drawer, hey?' remarked Sir Eustace Briggs. 'Ah! A very sensible place to keep it in, my boy. You could have no better place, in my opinion.'

And Trevor agreed with him, with the mental reservation that it rather depended on whom the drawer belonged to.

THE END

# TITLES IN THE COLLECTOR'S WODEHOUSE

Aunts Aren't Gentlemen
Barmy in Wonderland
Big Money
Bill the Conqueror
Blandings Castle
Carry On, Jeeves
The Clicking of Cuthbert
Cocktail Time
The Code of the Woosters
The Coming of Bill
A Damsel in Distress
Do Butlers Burgle Banks?
Doctor Sally
Eggs, Beans and Crumpets
A Few Quick Ones
Frozen Assets
Full Moon
Galahad at Blandings
A Gentleman of Leisure
The Girl in Blue
The Girl on the Boat
The Gold Bat
The Heart of a Goof
Heavy Weather
Hot Water
Ice in the Bedroom
Indiscretions of Archie
The Inimitable Jeeves
Jeeves and the Feudal Spirit
Jeeves in the Offing
Jill the Reckless
Joy in the Morning
Laughing Gas
Leave it to Psmith
The Little Nugget
Lord Emsworth and Others
Love Among the Chickens
The Luck of the Bodkins

The Man Upstairs
The Man with Two Left Feet
The Mating Season
Meet Mr Mulliner
Money for Nothing
Money in the Bank
Mr Mulliner Speaking
Much Obliged, Jeeves
Mulliner Nights
My Man Jeeves
Nothing Serious
The Old Reliable
A Pelican at Blandings
Piccadilly Jim
Pigs Have Wings
Plum Pie
The Pothunters
A Prefect's Uncle
Psmith in the City
Psmith, Journalist
Quick Service
Right Ho, Jeeves
Ring for Jeeves
Sam the Sudden
Service with a Smile
Something Fishy
Something Fresh
Spring Fever
Summer Lightning
Summer Moonshine
Thank You, Jeeves
Ukridge
Uncle Dynamite
Uncle Fred in the Springtime
Uneasy Money
Very Good, Jeeves!
Young Men in Spats